The Withdrawal

To Shane
Best wishes

A novel

by

Geoffrey Beevers

Geoffrey Beevers

fantom
publishing

First published in 2019 by Fantom Publishing, an imprint of Fantom Films
www.fantompublishing.co.uk

Copyright © Geoffrey Beevers 2019

Geoffrey Beevers has asserted his moral right to be identified
as the author of this work in accordance with the
Copyright, Designs and Patents Act 1988.

A catalogue record for this book is available from the British Library.

Hardback edition ISBN: 978-1-78196-342-5

Typeset by Phil Reynolds Media Services, Leamington Spa
Printed and bound by CPI Group (UK) Ltd, Croydon, CR0 4YY

Jacket design by Will Brooks

For my grandchildren, Joseph, Michael and Tristan

Also by Geoffrey Beevers and published by Fantom

THE FORGOTTEN FIELDS
THE PROGRESS ROAD
SUPERSEEDS

PREFACE

IN THE MID 2010s, I was sitting in a pub when a CCTV camera outside swivelled and looked through the window at me. I started to think about the parallels between our society and George Orwell's *1984*, and the germ of this book was born.

The novel is set in 2048, a hundred years after Orwell wrote his masterpiece, and is written partly in homage to it. On the surface, Orwell's target seems to be socialism, and mine consumerism; because the times are different. But the real target is the unrestrained power of a small minority. Such elites defend themselves by keeping their methods secret. The challenge is to bring them into the light, to identify the danger.

We already live in a consumer society in which a very few corporations gather information on us, through social media and the internet of things, which can be used to control our behaviour as consumers without our being able to do much about it. We don't fully understand how it works, but it understands how we work only too well. As a democracy, we need to get control of this; not only because there are issues – such as climate change – far more important than the need to support a consumer society in the interests of a few, but also because we risk losing fundamental freedoms to an unaccountable elite.

If we are so dependent on the technologies that others control, what would we do if all our smart technology were to be suddenly withdrawn from us? How would we survive?

This novel explores 'The Withdrawal'.

Geoffrey Beevers
July 2019

CHAPTER 1

IT WAS A HOT DAY IN MARCH, and the air was full of muffled chattering. In the square outside U-Chooz Plenty, men and women were gathering at lunchtime, many wearing brilliant primary colours. Almost everyone was on hand-screen, earnestly talking as if to themselves, self-absorbed, avoiding each other's eyes.

Alec had been in front of his work-screen all morning, in a darkened cubicle, and now the colour and bright sunlight were painful. To steady himself, he found himself sitting for a moment on one of the square's few benches, his back to the sun. He found his attention drawn away mindlessly to the energetic stream of commercials moving on the great screens around the square. There, at least, the beautiful people looked at him directly. He could feel the sun beating on his balding head, and he looked up. High above the crowds, on tall stems, UCTV cameras turned and paused, and turned again, unheeded, but eternally on safety watch. A traffic drone pulsed lightly overhead.

Guilt gave him the impetus to stand, and though he seemed to be feeling slightly sick, he followed the flow of the crowd into U-Chooz. Above the massive entrance, under the U-Chooz logo were the words:

CHOICE MAKES YOU FREE

Inside it was cooler. Other consumers flowed past him as he moved through the Food Hall, down the wide atrium, between the palm trees, each individual in a separate world. Sunshine flooded in from the glass arches in the roof far above, flooded into a space far wider and brighter than any mediæval cathedral, a space to inspire belief. Alec had no idea what he needed to buy, but was swept along in anticipation. Attracted almost automatically by the silver escalators, he allowed himself to be carried up into the glowing sunlight, while watery music played softly.

He found himself walking down a spacious concourse. He sometimes took this path at lunchtime. First the heavy smell of perfume, then the smell of fresh bread and coffee. At a counter, overflowing her two stools, a woman, substantial even by recent standards, was stuffing herself with an enormous doughnut. Normally he would stop here to get a sandwich and applejooz, but today he didn't feel quite up to it. Dimly, he felt he should get back to the Food Hall instead, so he decided to cut across through Fashion.

At the edge of the Fashion area, Alec had to pass down the Wedding Walk where all the bridal gear was on display. He had come here himself as a young man, to choose a wedding outfit for his bride. Even then, fifteen years ago, marriage was not considered significant; to stay together was a choice, of course, though not a very popular one, but the Wedding of Choice was always treated with the utmost seriousness. His wedding to Katherine had not been a spectacular affair by current standards, but it had seemed so to him at the time, and he was certain her family would still resent that part of their necessary debt. But Katherine had looked so beautiful in her traditional white gown and train. He remembered how deeply in love with her he had felt, and how he'd loved her strength balanced by her vulnerability, her ambitious nature tempered by her fear that she might not succeed. He remembered how committed he had felt to their future together, as she'd swept down the aisle to join him at the desk.

She had left him somewhat later, and only ever got in touch again when she wanted money for their baby daughter. As soon as he had set up an account for her, he had never seen either of them again… Well, just that once, by accident. He wondered if his wife might have had other children since. Somehow he doubted it. He had seen updates of her life for a while on U-Frendz; details of her developing career, her great success, and photos of her latest affairs; something once on U-Choob; but after a while he couldn't bear to look.

He had suffered a kind of breakdown in the end; a crisis of identity. He had tried to trace his ancestry, done all kinds of strange things, but eventually he'd settled down, come to terms. Except about his daughter.

Above all else, he still missed his daughter.

Towards the end of the Wedding Walk, there was a full-length mirror where girls could admire their outfits. A girl in a wedding dress was gazing at herself in complete self-absorption. Alec couldn't help seeing himself passing by, and stopped to study his reflection. He stood slightly behind the girl, and wondered if he would ever get married again. He saw his face give a slightly twisted smile, like a stranger's. Even under a thin beard, his face seemed abnormally hollow and lined for a man still in his forties, his body tall but slight, almost fading. He could never compete when everyone around him was so much bigger. Substantial was the current word.

Now, coming into the centre of Fashion, there was a heightened sense of excitement. The U-Katz fashion area was hung with the bright reds and yellows now so popular, dresses and shirts and underwear, often marked *Wear Once and Throw Away*. This was one of the few places where consumers seemed willing to leave the online world, and exchange surreptitious glances with strangers. The old slogan *Beware the Person – Trust the Screen* didn't seem to apply here. Alec couldn't help noticing a dark, plumpish girl in a short red outfit who suddenly looked directly at him, dropped her screen to her side and smiled. He realised he had seen her before, around his offices, where they had often passed in the corridor. She had never acknowledged him then, though he had an idea her name might be Sasha. He smiled back. Now she seemed to be flirting with him. She was holding up a yellow skirt against her body, as if to say 'What do you think?' But then a young man stepped forward from behind him, and Alec turned away in shock. He heard her voice.

'Don't you find buying things exciting?'

The cliché seemed to work. The young man followed her towards the changing rooms. These were supposed to double as virtual sex-booths for single occupancy, but were sometimes used by couples. It was part of the current fashion for the occasional 'real' experience. Alec couldn't help but watch, fascinated and strangely disturbed. The couple touched their cards on the pad, and entered the booth. The curtains didn't reach the floor, so Alec could see the girl's underwear drop around her ankles. Alec hated himself for standing there. Her legs parted. It was all over very quickly, while cameras watched them from above. When they emerged, the girl was wearing the yellow dress. As she wriggled to adjust her underwear, there was a little applause from one bystander, while another watched through his screen. Avoiding eye-contact, the couple went their separate ways.

Afterwards, there was a whirring sound as the booth cleaned itself with a damp cloth and disinfectant. Above the booth was a notice in large letters: *YOU CHOOSE*. And then, in smaller letters, *WARNING: The Real World Can Have Consequences*.

Alec wondered why it seemed to affect him so much. It wasn't normal to be angry. It was nothing to do with him; they were free individuals, it was their choice, they weren't hurting anyone, they were naturally excited by the whole consumer experience, it happened all the time – and yet he couldn't get out of his head the way the young man had patted the girl's shoulder in casual thanks as he left, and she had raised a hand in casual acknowledgement. He wanted to kick them to the ground and smash their heads together.

He moved on towards the Food Hall, cutting through by the old polling booths, which were now used as an assembly area for U-Chooz private security. In the old days, it was there

5

that you cast your vote in secret every five years for your favourite political personalities. Now, of course, your opinions were sampled online all the time, on every possible subject, which was much more democratic. The disused booths were half hidden by rows of security guards, with their tasers and automatics, ready to go anywhere in U-Chooz at the slightest sign of trouble. These really were substantial men, and Alec always felt comforted by their presence. He paused for a moment, and without quite knowing why, he felt obliged to check his screen for messages.

Soon he emerged above a bank of silver escalators, where he could see the vast Food Hall below, and the glass exit doors beyond. U-Chooz Plenty was like a city in itself, but it began and ended with the Food Hall, where everyone who wanted a real shopping experience could source all the food supplies they needed. But Alec was worried now that he needed to get back to work, to meet his targets, and he hurried down the escalator. He walked on very quickly between the shelves laden with vegetables from all over the world, and refrigerated units packed with tempting meals, where customers touched screens to compare prices or order deliveries. He came to the exit queue, his mind already occupied by the work he would need to do that afternoon. Then, as he pulled his card from his back pocket to put it in the slot, fear flushed through his whole body.

He had failed to buy a single thing, and it would be recorded on his card. His card might even be swallowed up, withdrawn.

How could he have been so stupid? He stepped away from the gates, and pushed his way back against the crowd, feeling horribly exposed. People muttered disapproval; cameras turned to follow him from above. He had never done such a thing before in his life. And this was the run-up to Summergreed when he should be more aware of these things. Instinctively, he looked for the nearest thing to pick up. There was a rack near the exit, full of toys and sweets to encourage children. He picked up a small teddy bear and rejoined the queue. There was another horrible moment, when his card disappeared into the slot, and a flood of relief when it re-emerged and the gate opened.

He went out into the hot sun, hugging his teddy bear. It was disgusting: small, red and rubbery.

Most of the time, of course, you took your card for granted. It was vital, since cash had been abolished. It monitored your salary, and all your payments, and told you the level of necessary debt you held. It was also an identity card, a passport, a detailed CV; it held all your medical records, and a host of other useful details. Along with your screen, which held your social life, it was the necessary accompaniment to your very existence. It was not unknown for people to lose their card, on occasion, and this could be very distressing, but U-Bank had all the information efficiently stored in the Cloud, and if you applied to the Retrieval Office, they could issue a replacement almost immediately.

Nevertheless, Alec sometimes had a recurring nightmare that he was guilty of some unspecified crime, and that the machines at the gates would swallow his card and his identity would be wiped out completely...

He knew it was unforgivable to go to U-Chooz and not spend anything at all. Why go to a shopping mall and not buy?

The gates had been reinstalled recently as a reminder, and to prevent antisocial behaviour. And yet, what punishment could there be for not spending? A fine perhaps? A visit to the corporate therapist? Alec had no idea. But surely they could never withdraw your card completely. The very thought was ridiculous, a worrying indication of the strange state of mind he could sometimes get into, a state of paranoia and exaggeration. Perhaps it came from rejection, and the loss of his daughter, something to do with the way his family had been withdrawn from him.

He mustn't get his fears out of proportion, thought Alec, as he checked his messages again, and then hurried back across the square to his work at the Info.

Alec could easily have worked from home, but he had chosen to work from an office, as a small minority of people did. After his wife had left, and after his breakdown, he had travelled abroad for a while. When he returned, his new flat had felt small and oppressive, and the thought of being there in front of his screen all day and night seemed too depressing. He knew it was more expensive, in fact almost pointless, to travel to work; but for him it was worth the effort, and gave him a sense of discipline he liked.

Across the square, he heard the ping as his card was recognised by Info reception, and then he took the lift to the 26th floor. His office was in Data Assessment, and was one of the cubicles with a window, but it was a solar window of the kind you couldn't see out of, so there was nothing to distract you from your screen. Alec felt himself lucky that, just before you reached his office, there was a recess in the corridor where the toilets were and which contained a drinks dispenser and a few chairs: this had an old-fashioned plate-glass window with a magnificent view over the city. He paused there now, and looked out for a moment. Though now one of the less significant cities in the globalised world, and as nothing compared with the great megacities of China, India or Brazil, London still had its fair share of great U-Chooz buildings. The one he was in was U-Chooz Information, or 'The Info' for short. It was the tallest, if you included the masts, and also the most slender, and covered all areas of knowledge, including news, education, entertainment and all information systems. The building he had just come from across the square was U-Chooz Plenty, sometimes known as the Hourglass. Dominating his view ahead, it tapered at first, like a great glass pyramid, terrace after terrace, stretching skywards, almost as far as he could see as he twisted his head to look up through the window. He had never explored beyond those retail floors of it, though he knew the tapered middle floors were for administration. After the slenderest point, the upper floors widened out again, and were for the provision of financial and banking services. But from where he stood, Alec could not see the upper floors.

Some distance away to the right, also dominating any other high-rise buildings for miles around, there was a third great tower. This was U-Chooz Safety, a great hexagonal block of concrete with small dark windows, which combined foreign affairs with home security. He knew nothing whatever about what went on there, though he assumed it was the nerve centre for our private security armies abroad, for arms manufacture and sales, and for all anti-terrorist operations. It was thought to penetrate as deep into the ground as it was high, but no one could ever get close to it because of permanent concrete walls in the streets, and security robots on guard.

There had once been a fourth great tower in the city, but this had been razed to the ground in a terrorist attack in the thirties. It had been known as 'The Government' and had once housed all the government ministries. Most of its functions had now been outsourced, or incorporated into the U-Chooz towers, especially after the sovereign debt crisis in the twenties, though there were smaller functions remaining, of which the biggest was in the old Taxation Building by the river, the one with the clock tower, which now provided public support for private corporations.

High on the U-Chooz building, almost opposite him, he could see the three great slogans of the democratic world, burning in huge letters.

CHOICE IS FREEDOM

GREED IS GREAT

ALL GROWTH IS GOOD

A moment later, the screen displayed the huge image of a half-naked girl tilted suggestively towards Alec, her short fair hair lazily over one eye. She turned her head slowly toward Alec and winked.

For a moment, in his loneliness, Alec felt the illogical warmth of inclusion.

At least she's not Big Brother, he thought wryly, as he hurried on down the corridor. A moment later, he was sitting at his desk, checking his screen.

As he propped his rubber teddy bear against the corner of his screen, Alec realised that he was at his happiest when he was working. In the Identification Unit of Data Assessment, there was an almost continuous stream of information coming his way. Mostly, of course, the U-Chooz algorithms could sort out individuals automatically, at a much faster rate than any army of bureaucrats. But every now and then the system seemed to be puzzled, and Alec would get a special assignment to sort something out, or double-check a decision.

In most cases, the screen collected the data of individuals to sell them on to the market. Their aim was to tell you what you wanted, before you knew you wanted it, to show you what sort of a person you were, to help you become more and more like a person of your type, and to see yourself as part of the global market. Most people could be steered into manageable boxes. Even rebellious types steered themselves into a manageable box – 'the type that likes to be different'. But occasionally there would appear to be a contradiction, an individual that U-Chooz servers couldn't work out. It was up to Alec to analyse this, to look in more depth at all the facets that made up the individual in question. Alec enjoyed this work. It was almost like being a psychologist as well as a detective. He sometimes wondered if he had been chosen for it, because they felt that he too was difficult to work out. But he certainly was good at resolving contradictions.

This afternoon he had waiting for him a message which read:

3.4.48Screen76743871UchlocalSW15daily,last2.4.48;Holtpsych 72943last23.3.48;med01379x47DBlast1.4.48;Chx

He had soon choozled the screen in question and was cleared for special access: the name, address, screen and card numbers. She was Helen, a young web-designer in the southwest of the city who had tried to shoplift from her local U-Chooz, and had registered for help with a corporate therapist, but for some reason, her medical records still did not match with her buying habits. Alec soon found the precise moment she had been typing to hack into her shopping records, to change them. Sometimes shame made people do these things. He also learnt that she worked from home, was five foot four inches, was morbidly substantial, kept two cats and had a limited sex-life, one same-sex partner five years ago who could be traced, but that wasn't necessary. Alec trawled through her clickstream, and followed some of her friendship sites. There were selfies from the past, one naked, and also recent footage of her going in and out of her house. He took a live update and found her driving to the doctors. But he had reached the limits of relevance in this case, and Alec wanted to respect her privacy. He reported back, as generously as he could, suggested she might need personal support from her U-Frendz and went on to the next case.

Alec knew he was not the only person doing this work. There were thousands of others in the Info alone, double-checking on people's lives, sometimes it seemed almost at random. They would check on the quality of others' work, target ads more precisely, look at crime, or keep an eye on eccentricities that might develop in indescribable directions. Paedophilia was always a problem, but thankfully he didn't have to look at unpleasant videos, which he passed on to a special unit. Terrorism was also a major worry, though he was never given a case directly. Perhaps he wasn't entrusted with such things, though he always flagged up any small suspicions he might have. Alec felt proud of the work he did, and loved the sense of the individual people emerging from a mass of data; he almost felt he was creating the individuals out of the information. Occasionally he wondered what became of his reports. Were they seen by more senior figures, or were they handled by algorithms in some massive impersonal network of servers, capable perhaps of making the subtlest decisions? He would probably never know.

Now he was being asked to run checks on an official because of a fault in some entry gates at a food distribution warehouse which had failed to record the arrival of four lorry-loads. The mistake here turned out to be a technical glitch in the operating system which was quickly autocorrected. Alec wondered what sanctions there might have been if the official had been at fault. He suspected that in most cases U-Chooz took no action at all. They just liked to keep informed. The whole system was almost self-policing; with so much inform-ation flowing upwards, nobody liked to step out of line.

*

He often wondered if he might come across his daughter during the course of his work. It was obviously forbidden to use his work-time to pursue private matters, or indeed to pursue actively any member of the public without special clearance from above. And Katherine had gone to great lengths to deny him any access, or even knowledge, of his daughter. But he couldn't help wondering, when he saw a young girl caught in a drunken brawl by accident, or watched some enquiry into an Academy exam, if that dark girl on camera there, who was about the right age, might not be her. But the truth was, he could never know for certain. How could he tell what she would look like now? How could he know anything but her name, Alice, which Katherine might well have changed? He could of course easily trace Katherine from his personal screen, and humble himself to her; but he was prevented by pride and dread and disgust. His only hope was that his daughter might one day, when she was grown up, want to trace her father. It would be a much easier prospect for her; but so far she had shown no signs of wanting to do so.

Meanwhile, it was painful to think that the central servers knew more about Alice than he could ever know. Cameras could watch her as she ran down the street, Chooz-U-Flix could tell which films she enjoyed; Medichex knew what medicines she needed, U-Chooz knew all her favourite colours, what takeaways she preferred, what teddy bear lay on her pillow. The teddy bear itself might even be watching her sleep. All this information was held separately in the Cloud, and would only be put together if U-Chooz saw a special need for it. But they saw no need, as he did. No, he would have to wait on her decisions. But sometimes the desire to see her again, to talk with her about her life, to see if she remembered him, was almost overwhelming, it was so sharp and painful.

Sometimes he wondered if his memories of Alice might be exaggerated, the vivid memories of those first months, the waxy smell of her baby head, feeding her from the bottle because Katherine didn't want to breastfeed. He would walk her up and down in the sleepless nights humming Brahms' lullaby to make her sleepy, and later he would read picture books like *The Gruffalo* to her, take her to the swings, play with her during the long days when Katherine was constantly at work. She had contained all his hopes for the future.

It must be thirteen or more years now since Katherine had left. He had watched from the first-floor window of their flat, as she opened the car door and looked back up at him, holding the three-year-old in her arms. Her eyes were bright with scorn and hatred. The child was asleep, sound asleep at a moment when she could not have known what was happening to her. Now she was being strapped into the back seat of the car. He was slow to understand, but Katherine was taking his baby, their baby. She slammed the car door viciously, went round to the driving seat, didn't bother to look up again, she never looked back, she just drove off in their car. With their child.

He had searched for them in vain. Till, two years later, he had been walking down some distant street in a seaside town. He could still feel the shock of seeing Katherine, moving away ahead of him, the slight sway of her hips unmistakeable, a little figure at her side, still clutching a fluffy doll at her waist. He could hear his own voice calling 'Alice!' but it was Katherine who was turning, recognising him, her face hardening. Now the girl was turning too. Those big dark eyes.

He had stopped, staring at her. He could hear her small voice:

'Who's that, Mummy?' ... and the answer:

'That's nobody.'

The mother was pulling the child onward. Then she was picking her up, lifting her on to her hip, breaking into a run. Alice was still looking back at him. She tried again – 'Mummy?' – but if there was a reply, he couldn't hear it. He was standing there in shock, unable to move. They were disappearing over the crest of a hill, bobbing away down the other side. Alice was still staring at her father, as she disappeared from sight. And he knew that, though he loved his daughter beyond all understanding, he'd probably never see her again.

That was many years ago now. His inner life had hardly moved on since. Perhaps the concept of an inner life was meaningless anyway. He could hope for reunion with his daughter one day, possibly, though he sometimes felt that even that hope had become fossilised and unreal. But beyond that? His experience with Katherine had not given him confidence with women. It was true, he did sometimes yearn for some kind of intimacy. Yes, that was it. Some private intimacy. Perhaps within a family. Today everything had to be shared publicly onscreen.

And today it seemed you were obliged to share only your own managed self-image, your perfect life, your photoshopped looks, and your own individual excitements, sex and greed. There were no real relationships admitted, no deep or complex sorrows.

He found himself staring at the red teddy bear propped against his screen, which looked blankly back at him with its fixed rubber grin.

CHAPTER 2

ALEC WAS IN THE CHESTNUT WINE BAR across the square, sitting at a table by the window, with the teddy bear and a Choozacola in front of him. He knew he had to get more recorded spending on his card before the end of the day, or he would feel vaguely sinful. Everyone was expected to do their bit for economic growth. It was early, and there were only a handful of others in the bar, all at separate tables, working at screens or talking to screens or even staring blankly through U-Glasses. He didn't want to look at them directly. Out in the square, the sun had lost its heat, and the moving screens on the face of the Info were standing out more brightly.

Suddenly the screens across the square faded to black. Alec looked round and the screens in the wine bar were fading too. He had a sense that everyone was looking up in a sudden stillness. After a moment the words *Breaking News* appeared, and an announcer declared: 'The terrorist alert has been raised from Yellow to Orange. Please be alert, film anything suspicious, keep your purchases with you, we will update you.'

This announcement was followed by pictures of drone strikes, and devastated towns where not one building stood whole, and deserts where some unnamed battle was being fought. There were pictures of eager young security soldiers firing, and of enemy dead, while the commentator talked of our boys who had bravely given their lives. A private security officer, Ogilvie, was singled out for his courage and dedication, his loyalty to his comrades, his good sense of humour.

Then, without warning, a picture of the Caliph came up on the screen. A groan of hatred rippled round the bar; Alec heard a strange sound in his own throat before he realised what it was. For a brief moment, eyes met in agreement across the bar, and among a few isolated individuals grew a strange, rare moment of solidarity. It was always the same picture you saw. The Caliph's face was ordinary enough – you could almost understand how people could be taken in by him – and yet here was the man responsible for hundreds of thousands of innocent deaths. Vilified a thousand times a day onscreen, his theories ridiculed for the evil rubbish they were, his influence never seemed to grow less. He was the commander of a vast shadowy army, an underground network of conspirators, dedicated to the overthrow of the Free World, and the triumph of 'The Book'. He was almost a mythical figure, and though he might even be long dead, his supporters believed he had ascended into heaven, and he still represented a focus for people's hope or hatred.

Alec looked out into the square. In a gathering crowd, he could see a man spit viciously, and a woman with fishlike protuberant eyes was staring angrily. Others were suddenly shouting, or gesturing at the screen.

After a couple of minutes, the newsflash ended abruptly and the screen went back to advertising normality. First was the half-naked girl with the fair hair over one eye who was turning slowly towards Alec.

A figure at his shoulder made him jump.

'Dreadful worry, isn't it? Another Orange Alert.'

Alec recognised a substantial man from further down his corridor at the Info, whom he saw sometimes at the drinks dispenser. He wore with pride the yellow smart-badge that they all wore at U-Chooz to monitor their physical movements. His name was Simon.

'That bastard Caliph.' Alec remembered that when Simon got excited he showered a fine mist of spittle till the froth gathered at the corners of his mouth. Then he wiped this away neatly with his thumb and forefinger.

'I'm wondering,' he confided, 'how much longer I can keep up this business of working where we do. It would be so much easier to work from home and I swear that travelling to the City centre gets more dangerous every day.' He looked mournfully into the square.

'It's good for reality shopping,' returned Alec dutifully, gesturing towards U-Chooz Plenty.

'That's true.' Simon paused and then brightened. 'That reminds me, have you tried the new razors?'

Alec's heart sank as Simon touched his smart-badge and then took an electric razor from his pocket.

There seemed to be only two excuses for conversation these days: one was to sympathise about the terrorist situation, the other was to get excited about a new product. You could make a few extra credits from U-Chooz if you would personally recommend some product you genuinely liked. And it wasn't hard to feel genuine if you needed the credits. Alec was trying to maintain an expression of interest, though he couldn't believe Simon was supporting such an old-fashioned product without the slightest novelty or technological edge to it. Why not the latest screen game or 3D printer?

Simon was saying, 'People will always need to shave,' and Alec had a strange sense that Simon would not be long for this world. 'They've got seven special rotating blades, can you imagine? More blades than ever before, for a smoother than ever shave. It's wonderful, really makes me want to get up in the morning. If you don't mind me saying, you look as if you could really benefit from one of these.'

Alec rubbed his chin and felt the untidiness of his beard.

'Yes, thank you for the tip, I might do that.'

'Treat yourself for Summergreed!' grinned Simon, returning the razor to his pocket.

'How's work?' said Alec, trying to change the subject.

'I seem to get freeloaders mainly,' said Simon, 'trying to get away without pulling their weight. They should be castrated and shot in my opinion.'

'Mmm,' said Alec noncommittally. Conversations about work were usually kept to such mundane generalities.

'Well, I'd better leave you to it,' said Simon, indicating the screen which Alec was idly turning in his hands. 'I'm going to get something to eat.' And he was off to get a Choozburger from the bar. But then he turned back for a brief last word. 'Oh, do look me up online – I'm trending right now – my following's growing. You should see the selfie of me shaving in the morning.'

Alec stared out of the window. He couldn't help over-hearing two girls at a nearby table talking about their purchases in high piercing voices. They were talking to their screens, of course, not to each other. But the range of expression seemed to be getting narrower, thought Alec. No one was consciously manipulating the language, but there were certain thoughts it was hard to share. There were certain people and things it was almost impossible to criticise in public, others you couldn't praise. You were free to think anything of course. Thought is free. You could think *The terrorist threat is overrated*, or even *U-Chooz could be wrong*. But Alec felt cold the moment that dissident counter-thought passed through his mind. Such thoughts expressed could only be met with horror and incomprehension.

At that moment, his guilty glance met the eye of a man sitting by himself at a table in the far corner, who gave him a half-smile before returning to his glass of wine. Alec felt a flash of sympathetic recognition pass between them. Surely this man hadn't been there a moment ago. He was strongly built, with the look of someone successful and cultural, and with sharply intelligent grey eyes. Kind eyes too, Alec thought, not a hint of cruelty. He had a strange feeling he had seen him somewhere before, but couldn't remember where. He knew the moment of connection was somehow significant. Who was this man?

But across the square the screens were growing ever more bright and demanding in the growing gloom. I must go home, Alec thought. He checked his messages again, but there was nothing, and he wasn't really expecting anything. He was beginning to drain what was left in his cola glass when the screens outside dipped again. Everyone turned.

Breaking News; and the announcer began: 'Figures for the last quarter have just been released. They show economic growth has risen in line with U-Chooz profits. Stock markets are up. Inflation remains under control.' There were appreciative murmurs and cheers from the bar. Alec paused to take in the detailed figures. They were encouraging. The long recovery continued. Over the years there had been economic crises, but then U-Chooz would impose tax and spending cuts and they would pump in more money to U-Bank, and the economy would grow again. It was wonderful how well the markets were working, thought Alec, and felt relieved.

But there was another strange counter-thought. You could share quite easily the idea 'Economic growth is the key to happiness'. It was almost a religious belief. But to question it, or to ask, 'What exactly is it that's growing?' would make no sense to anyone. He immediately censored himself for his stupidity, and yet found himself glancing across to the corner of the bar. But the man had already gone.

He looked out of the window again, and by now the news was ending with the standard declaration *U-Chooz Newz is Certified U-True* before the screens had returned to their usual advertising mode. Again there was the half-naked girl with fair hair over one eye. She turned towards Alec and slowly winked.

He picked up the rubber teddy bear.

It was time to go home.

*

The same image of the half-naked girl was on the escalators down to the tube. As you went down, she took off her top, and by the time you reached the bottom, she was completely naked. Then she winked.

There had once been a debate about whether such ads were exploiting women. They were certainly exploiting his sexuality, Alec thought, which was definitely stirring as he reached the foot of the escalator. He somehow hated the girl for it. He wondered what the ad was for. U-Braz perhaps. In the old days it had mattered what ads were for. But it had long been decided that as far as public screens were concerned, to incite people to spend more was more important than the individual product, as a general atmosphere of acquisition would benefit all companies in the end. So now most public screens concentrated on selling sex and greed, and the product was rarely mentioned, but was left to the free choice of the individual. Only on individual screens were ads tightly targeted.

The train was in a filthy state, but not overcrowded, now that most people worked from home. The company that ran it was, unusually, not a U-Chooz subsidiary, and had been putting in little investment, hoping to be bought up by them. It also suffered the disadvantage of being a public space, because everyone was fearful of terrorist attack. The customers stared at their screens and most looked lost and depressed. But Alec didn't mind the journey; it only took fifteen minutes to his home stop, and from there it was only a short walk home.

Outside the tube was a rare local U-Chooz, where all he could think to buy was a bottle of their water. Up the hill, Alec hesitated, and then sat for a moment on a bench facing the road, a little breathless, realising how unfit he was. Behind him was the Personal Improvement Centre in an old disused church, where people went for a spiritual moment. Alec sometimes dropped in, but he didn't feel like it tonight. You could express your deepest desires there on a screen positioned at the altar end. It was claimed by spiritual people that you could have anything in life if you wanted it enough, and many confessed to the screen their desire for a new house, or car, or for a better-paid job. Alec had once asked 'to see my daughter', but nothing had happened so he hadn't tried it again. Perhaps his desire hadn't been practical enough: you couldn't exactly buy it. It was getting darker as he sat on the bench, and he began to feel strangely depressed, so he moved on quickly.

He told his screen to have his meal ready and soon arrived at the modern gated development that was his home. He used his card to get in through the iron gates, then again to enter his block, but the front door of his flat recognised his face automatically. And as soon as he opened the door, the lights came up in his hallway; he could see through to his living room, where the home screen lit up, and he felt better as a soft voice said:

'Hello Alec. Welcome Home.'

*

He spent the rest of the evening as most people would, married or single. He turned one of his walls into a view of some trees. He then took his heated ready-meal from the meal dispenser, and ate in front of the screen, catching up on the latest news. Abroad, progress was being made. Soon our forces could be withdrawn to move on to another country where our help was needed more. Millions were being displaced, but they couldn't come here without the right card or screen. Some pictures were distressing. It was sometimes difficult to tell the reality from the video war-games being advertised, but the message was basically the same. Given time and practice the game was definitely winnable.

The economic news was encouraging too. Just another push on spending, and profits would rise yet further. It was all part of the build-up to Summergreed, thought Alec, when big discounts would be available.

After his meal, Alec stayed in front of his screen. This was now his own time. For half an hour he was comparing prices for the services he received. This had to be done every day, or he would lose out on the bargains and savings and free gifts. In a pause, a quiet voice prompted him: 'Would you like to check on your Frendz?' So for another hour he checked up on his networks. Everybody naturally belonged to a friendship group where you could tell everybody about your day. He did this on U-Frendz. Everybody had a hate group where you could sound off in the most revolting language you could devise. U-Hate was fun. He gave his thoughts on the girl in the ad, and felt better. He got an almost instant response from U-Hate-Women which he decided Not To Like.

He checked up on 'The Diggers'. This was a group set up to question and challenge. They had called themselves 'The Diggers' because they liked to dig a little deeper into public issues. The influencer was a woman calling herself Cally. He had tried for a while to establish some closer connection with her, but she and most of the other interesting voices seemed to have disappeared, and the group had deteriorated lately into just another hate group, so he hardly visited the site any more. Groups formed and dissolved so quickly, it was hard to keep track. He checked his popularity ratings, found a few hits on his site, but nothing from his daughter. He updated his site info, but in a rather half-hearted manner. He saw his social credit scores were sinking, and he knew he didn't try hard enough, but the competition was so intense. Finally, prompted by his screen, he checked his finances; he was only just over a hundred thousand in debt he discovered. He might have to borrow more. He always worried about his debt, but it was no worse than anybody else's, and though the interest piled up, nothing serious ever seemed to happen. How could it? U-Chooz had the economy firmly under control.

About eleven o'clock he felt exhausted, and his eyes stung from staring at the screen. He clicked on a few personalised ads, and followed their trails, mostly out of a sense of duty. He'd like to have watched a film to unwind, perhaps the remix of an old classic, or even a romcom like *Chooz-Me-Do*, recently enhanced with extra product placement, but he felt too tired now. There were never enough hours in the day.

And then he found himself thinking of the man whose eye he had caught in the Chestnut. He felt certain that the man was a senior figure, in finance perhaps. He seemed to have seen, or dreamt, that look before. So intelligent, slightly amused. And there was that hint of rebellion in his eyes, often involved in eye-to-eye contact. It was odd, but he liked it.

But what was there to rebel against? There were two interconnected things that ruled the rhythms of his life: his card and his screen. His card provided him with access to his home, his work, his shopping, his food, his whole life. The screen in front of him, with its extension, his hand-screen, was his gateway to all friendship, knowledge, music, all social opportunity. As much as he understood his screen, it understood him equally. It knew all his needs and provided them. This surely was a form of intimacy. It was not exactly private, admittedly. But he was a free man, free to do exactly as he liked. He wasn't a slave to his screen. If he didn't like the Diggers, or U-Hate-Women, or anything else about the screen, he could avoid it.

He could, if he felt like it, convey his most rebellious counter-thoughts to paper, say; there was nothing to stop him. He could choose to write an old-fashioned diary if he wanted. He could write *This war is wrong* or *Economic Growth is Rubbish* or *We're heading for Extinction* and nothing would happen. He could write five times over, in big capitals, *FUCK U-CHOOZ* and no one would mind. Provided he did his bit for the economy, no one would take any notice. So what was the point? In fact that would be a little ridiculous. Nobody wrote down anything like that any more. All thoughts were onscreen anyway, and the screen could provide for everything.

He was still staring at it abstractedly, when he was startled by a knock on the door.

*

There was a blonde woman at the door. Alec recognised her as the woman who owned the flat across the hallway. She looked nervous.

'I'm so sorry to bother you so late, but I'm a bit worried. Can I ask you...?'

She peered round Alec as if she was trying to see something behind him. Alec couldn't remember ever having spoken to her before. He had no idea of her name. She was far shorter than him, and he felt uneasy, so close to her, looking down into her hair. It was dyed, very fair; he couldn't help looking at the darker roots.

She looked up at him. 'I'm frightened. You see, the children…'

Her sentences seemed to drift off into uncertainty. He remembered she had two children, tubby twin boys of about nine or ten. He saw them from his bedroom window some mornings, on their way to the local Academy. Only three days a week now, since the Academies were being phased out in favour of virtual teachers and 'onscreen learning in the home environment'. Although on the surface well-behaved, the twins seemed to give off an air of permanent discontent.

She was peering round him again. 'Are your screens working?'

'Of course,' said Alec, standing aside, so she could see the comforting gleam from the living room.

'Mine have gone dark.' She looked up appealingly, and there was fear in her eyes. 'Only I know you work with screens. At least I gathered…' She must have been about fifty, but there wasn't a line on her face. 'Could you possibly…' she said. Injections, he was thinking.

Alec went with her to her flat. It turned out to be much larger than his one-bedroom apartment. This was probably one of the three-bedroom ones, very clean and spare of detail, just white walls and screens. The twins were sitting on a leather discount sofa, staring discontentedly at a huge black wall-screen. A small robotic teddy beside them was repeating mindlessly, 'Come and watch, come and watch…'

'What are we going to *do*?' the boys whined, kicking the sofa in unison with their feet. 'We want to kill Osama…'

'I shouldn't worry,' he said, trying to look reassuring. The children turned as one, and stared at him with instant distrust and suspicion in their eyes, almost as if they were personally blaming him. He knew there was very little help he could give. He knew nothing at all about how screens worked; only a few expensive specialists did, and the screens were all built into the walls, so there were no parts you could look at without taking the house to pieces. He supposed he could check that the autocorrect button had been reset. As he went to do so, she talked on.

'Only the children were playing *Terror Wars* and they'd just got to the compound to kill Osama, and now they can't. And I'd promised them that when they'd killed him, they could have…'

At that moment, all around the flat, the screens came on of their own accord, with a clatter of gunfire from the main screen.

'Oh, what a relief,' she said. 'I've never known that happen before.'

The children ran round him, whooping and screaming, 'It's *Terror Wars*! We're going to kill you!' before returning to the sofa. 'Kill you, kill you!' repeated the robotic teddy mindlessly; and then more softly to Alec, 'Who is your Mummy? Where do you live?'

Alec ignored the toy, and answered the woman.

'It is unusual,' he said, 'but the system always mends itself, so it never lasts long. There's a back-up, and back-ups behind that. You can never lose information, as they say.' Alec suddenly noticed the living-room curtains were half-drawn, and he found himself looking out of the window into the darkness.

The woman became apologetic. 'Yes, the flat is very nice, but it faces the wrong way...' She went to close the curtains. 'I'm thinking of moving as soon as I can afford to upgrade, but it's not always easy.' Alec could see what she meant about facing the wrong way. Over the wall of their enclave, you could see the lights in the tower blocks where the underclass lived. At that moment, in the distance beyond, there was a flash in the darkness, then the dull thud of an explosion, and soon the whine of a security siren. Or possibly an ambulance. Behind him, explosions from the children's screengame echoed the violence in the streets.

He still stood looking out, idly watching two or three fat mosquitos sitting on the other side of the glass. It must be the increasing warmth of the climate, he thought, that made them so numerous and so fat. But the woman was waiting, her hand on the curtain, her voice harder now, dismissing him.

'Thank you so much for coming.'

He looked down at her unlined face. No, not injections, but surgery, he thought. The face was altering now, as a new anxiety crept over it, the fear of a stranger lingering in her living space. Back on the sofa, the children were looking at him with undisguised hatred. It was time to go. Alec backed away, looking for the door. A moment later, he was rapidly retreating across the hallway to his own apartment. Behind him he heard the twins' whispered insult, hissed in unison at him, and it struck him as sharply as a stone to the back of his head.

'Osama!'

As they went back to their game, he could hear a clatter of machine-guns from their screen.

*

It was not surprising, Alec thought, that children were taught to suspect strangers, and report anything suspicious. They'd had a typical middle-class upbringing, were going to a sponsored Academy, and had been properly taught individual entitlement. They would have been told not to welcome strangers from any apparently different background, even from across the hallway, as such a person could so easily be a terrorist, or worse. It was only natural. *Beware the person, trust the screen.* He had been brought up that way himself at a very privileged school. He agreed with it. Almost. And yet, as sometimes happened, another way of thinking seemed to knock at his inner mind.

To settle himself, he sat down again in front of his screen. He clicked on several ads, then saw a nice pair of shoes on U-Buy and ordered them. His screen said: *If you like them, why not order two pairs?*, so he did. Then it seemed he had won a small prize in a lottery draw. This was better. He felt back on track. He was interrupted by a message from a group called The Watch, who were gathering a flash mob together to attack a paedophile's house very near him. Only to jeer and throw stones at the windows, it was stressed. He felt he should join in, but suddenly felt tired. Perhaps his public spirit had been exhausted by responding to the woman across the hall.

For some reason, stung by the children's insult perhaps, he choozled 'Osama'. Alec felt he didn't look remotely like him, except that he had a beard, a much less impressive one. And then he looked up 'The Caliph', and there was the hateful picture. He followed some links till he stumbled over some unpleasant videos. There seemed to be nothing to stop him. He was surprised the freedom of the net extended so far. But after watching for a while he could understand why. It was such unpleasant viewing, bombs exploding, violent speeches, public executions, he could not imagine this being very effective in recruiting people to the cause. Then he was asked if he wanted to buy a gun. At least the twins' game had only been a reconstruction; this was reality and surely anyone could tell the difference, even nowadays. He felt disgusted. It was time to go to bed.

In the night he had uneasy dreams. One of them was a recurring one. He was standing in front of a tribunal of judges. They all wore white robes, and shone like angels. The chief judge had a soft voice and told him, in the kindest manner, that because he was inadequate, he must put his card into a special slot in front of him. When he did so, a black mouth in the machine swallowed his card, and the judge explained gently: 'This is the Withdrawal. Now your card has been withdrawn, you no longer have a soul.' Then he found himself sliding naked down a chute, into some terrible underworld where dark figures with milky protuberant eyes stared at each other constantly in fear and hatred, and he knew he was one of those without souls, doomed to wander without hope for ever.

Unusually, during the night, he had to go twice to the toilet. Just as he settled down to sleep the second time, a soft voice from the screen said:

'Are you not sleeping well?'

He didn't bother to reply. After a moment it said gently, 'Would you like a sleeping pill?' Another pause. 'Or would you rather watch a movie?'

'Shut up,' he said.

'Choice is Free,' said the screen, almost sadly, and fell silent.

After that, he seemed to lie for hours, somewhere between drowsing and sleeping. The only light came from his screen, which could never be turned off completely, but very dimly continued to broadcast a choice of commercials or soft porn all night, or played soothing music. Alec was eventually able to turn over and close his eyes.

Then he dreamed again. In his dream, he was standing at the drinks dispenser near his office, looking out of the window, looking across at U-Chooz Plenty, the Hourglass. A few storeys higher than him, a man was standing at a window, looking down at him. It was the man in the Chestnut at the far corner table who had caught his eye. The man raised a hand as if in acknowledgement. Even across the square, Alec had the idea that they might have known each other as children, and that his name was Brian something. *Don't worry*, the man seemed to be reassuring him, *I am with you, I understand all your needs and fears. We shall meet up soon. We shall meet*, he seemed to say, *in the place where the screens are silent.* Had he said screens, or was it screams? In the half-state between sleeping and waking, Alec seemed to puzzle about that for a long time. No, they would meet in the place where the screens were silent.

Then a new counter-thought entered his mind: *Beware the screen, trust the person.*

When he woke next it was already morning.

CHAPTER 3

THE BUILD UP TO SUMMERGREED was not a happy time for Alec. His Frendz all seemed to be obsessed by what they were going to buy. They seemed to know just what they wanted, and were terribly enthusiastic about showing their presents off to each other. Sasha down the corridor was apparently going to buy herself a huge supply of organic chocolate; Simon was to get a number of tins of shaving gel which he generously intended to share among his Frendz. Alec knew he had to choose, but he found it difficult. A new hand-screen perhaps? He knew it needed upgrading but he was sort of happy with the old one. He found it all strangely burdensome. In the old days you bought presents for other people, and they bought presents for you, but then slowly it was felt to be more reliable if people bought the presents they wanted for themselves. It was easy to have the thought *I must pamper myself, I need to buy something*, but the counter-thought would sometimes enter his head *I don't need to buy anything for myself.* He knew it was unsociable, almost criminal, like saying 'the whole economy can go to hell'. But all around him the frenzy seemed to grow, and it made him uncomfortable.

His Hate Group was getting more and more excitable too, focusing for the moment on illegals. The raised level of security made everyone feel less secure on the streets, and only five weeks before the start of Summergreed there was a bomb on the tube.

Alec had been on the line back from town in the evening, when the train unaccountably stopped in the tunnel. There was a long delay before the driver announced that they were held because of a terrorist incident ahead of them. People began to glance at each other with growing unease. After half an hour, a man further down the carriage suddenly started screaming in short bursts of panic, and Alec, like many others, put his fingers in his ears to try to blot out the sound. No one helped the man of course: *Beware the person...* But Alec could feel the horror that everybody felt, of being utterly trapped and alone.

Eventually the train started to inch forward in spasms, till it reached the next station. There was devastation in the exit where a suicide bomber had struck, and security personnel were everywhere. They were hurried past the worst of the mess, everybody connecting noisily with their screens. On the way up the stairs, there was a streak of red amidst a pile of brick and dust, and a plaster-white severed hand. Alec knocked the thing out of the way with his foot, as he pressed on upwards. He had to push through a throng of bystanders, on their screens, uploading pictures of the carnage. Once at street level, he managed to duck under a police cordon and slip unnoticed down a side street, where relief flooded through him. Casual suicide bombs were a constant hazard of the Permanent War, but Alec had never been so close to its effects before.

After that day, the tube had been closed for three days, and Alec had to work from his personal screen at home, which he disliked.

Once, during this time, trying to escape the claustrophobia he felt at home, Alec found himself wandering in the Underclass Area, which he had not done for years. To the south and east of his gated area of expensive flats, the underclass lived in vast public estates, mostly built in concrete blocks or towers about eighty years ago, in the 1960s or '70s, and now dangerous and sometimes given to collapse. He tried to avoid going among these, and at first kept to the wider streets. There were not many people about: a young veteran without legs pushing himself along in a wheelchair, looking at the screen in his lap; an old woman trailing along with some shopping, listening to her earpiece; a group of young men exchanging drugs on a street corner. He couldn't help trying to imagine what it must be like to be one of these people. Two drunks in the street were arguing furiously, almost coming to blows. He noticed there seemed to be more safety cameras here, but less control.

As he ventured deeper into the area, he felt more out of his depth. Once he saw a piece of graffiti scrawled on the wall. In his part of town the graffiti said things like *To be Me is to be Free, To be Free is to Chooz* or *Don't think For yourself, think Of yourself*, but this one just said:

NEVER TAKE US FOR GRANTED

It was slightly disconcerting.

Soon he was drawn down a small side street by the sight of an old pub sign and went in. He realised how much some part of him longed for human communication, and though he was slightly disgusted at himself, he felt he needed to talk to someone. He didn't like to talk directly to any of the women there, so he bought a pint and tried to place himself somewhere obliquely across from a young man who was staring into his beer.

He tried some general remark like, 'How's it going?'

Two hollow eyes turned directly at him. He winced. 'What do you think?' the man said aggressively, and then went into a long monologue which Alec could barely understand. He caught some of it, something about his work and the hours and contracts and debts and how he'd never have anything of his own. 'But who cares? Nobody!' He hardly seemed to notice when Alec extricated himself and slipped away.

Alec then tried sitting near a very old white man in a corner, with whom he finally managed to strike up a conversation. Curious, he asked him what the past had been like. He offered to buy the man a pint, and when the man accepted, felt he had to buy a second pint for himself too, though he wasn't used to drinking at all.

The old man wasn't very forthcoming, talking while still watching the pub screen, or the screen in his hand. He'd lived in London most of his life, had muddled memories of the old NHS, and had been to something called a 'comprehensive'. What was it like in those days, Alec asked, before U-Chooz took over responsibility? Was life hard?

The old man simply shrugged. 'Well, it's just life, innit…'

Alec had always imagined the past was a grey world of government interference and wasteful bureaucracy, where health and safety ruled everything and business was regulated out of existence, where political correctness dominated, and minorities and immigrants were favoured beyond all reason. He put the idea to the old man.

'I dunno about that. I remember the foreigners buying up the football clubs. That's when football got too expensive to go to.'

'But isn't it better anyway onscreen?' Alec asked.

'Not if you're a Chelsea supporter,' was the reply. 'Haven't won a match in months.' After a while he went on, mysteriously, 'I blame the robots…'

Alec was confused. Did he mean robots on the pitch, or in the stands, or what?

'Now, bugger off,' the old man said, and went back to watching the screen.

Alec became aware that others were beginning to stare at him, sensing a stranger in their midst. Someone called over, 'What are you after? What are you doing here?' Alec rose and retreated quickly.

He came out of the pub feeling muddled, and a little drunk, a very odd sensation for him. Without knowing where he was going, he turned a corner and almost immediately felt the street he was in was strangely familiar, though he couldn't think why. There was a long row of square concrete shops, some of them boarded up, including the branch of a long-gone bank, or could it even have been a post office? Most of the shops that were left seemed to be gambling shops, or pawn shops, or cheap stores with everything under ten pounds. There were rough sleepers in the doorways. And then, at the far end of the street there was an even older building, a

Victorian bookshop with a small wooden sign outside it: *Julie's Bookshop*. How extraordinary, Alec thought. He used to go to bookshops like this very occasionally to find children's books for Alice. It was rare to see physical books nowadays, but as he approached, he saw there were some in the window, yellowed by sunlight. They looked as if they hadn't been touched for years. Alec was fascinated and found himself going in.

Inside there were bookshelves from floor to ceiling, packed with paperbacks, but all seemed dusty and undisturbed. There were no customers in the shop, only a roundish woman, perhaps a little older than he was, behind a counter, and a young girl of about twenty sorting through a pile of books on a table, in a narrow space towards the back of the shop.

'May I look around?' he said.

'Of course you may,' said the woman. What was that accent, Alec wondered? She had an unusually genuine smile.

He looked at the titles on the shelves, while she watched him with curiosity from the counter. He supposed customers were very rare. There were many classics there from the nineteenth and twentieth centuries: Eliot, Tolstoy, Kafka, Huxley; not so many after about 2030 of course, because very few people bought books except as downloads from Choozabook. He took down a copy of *Brave New World* but became self-conscious with the woman's eyes on him, and after a moment he put it back. At last he said:

'You must be Julie.'

She grinned cheerfully. 'That's right.'

He found himself disconcerted by that direct, friendly gaze. But then he was not used to the Underclass Area. He looked away, feeling slightly shifty, but with the memory of those direct brown eyes and that open smile in his mind. She wasn't even carrying a screen.

The girl at the back of the shop started singing quietly, some sort of a folk song. She obviously worked at the shop, and might well be Julie's daughter.

'There are more books upstairs if you want to look.'

He followed Julie up the narrow staircase. There were two more rooms upstairs, one at the front and one at the back of the house. Each room had books from floor to ceiling. The old Victorian floorboards were covered with a few worn pieces of carpet. He went into the room at the back, which had a bed and an old chair with a throw over it to disguise its failings. An antique clock made an odd ticking sound. Julie stayed while he quietly looked through some of the titles on the bookshelves. The sounds of the city seemed very far away. Dust floated in the sunlight from the window. There was a small screen in the room, but it looked so old-fashioned he doubted if it was even a standard two-way affair. He didn't feel at all watched, except by Julie.

'Beautiful place you have here,' he said.

'Yes, it belongs to a Mr Charrington. The books are all his, but he's very old now and has lost all interest in the place. He lets me run it for him.' Then she pulled a wry face. 'But we don't sell very much.'

'How do you manage?'

'Oh, we get by. Sometimes I let out this room for rent, and then I job-share with some friends. Or we exchange our time. Mostly, I look after children. Always lots of children who need looking after round here. I do cleaning work too, but I've always liked children best.'

Alec was thinking, *I'd like to rent this room, come here often, escape from my life, start all over again.* But he knew it was only an absurd counter-thought, so he said nothing and carried on browsing. There was a selection of children's books by the window and he couldn't help noticing *The Gruffalo*, a particular favourite of his that he used to read to Alice. She had loved the pictures.

'I'm Alec, by the way,' he said, sounding rather formal even to himself. She seemed amused.

'Pleased to meet you, Alec,' she said and gave a mock curtsey.

'I'd like to buy this one,' he said at last, taking the copy of *The Gruffalo* from the shelf, and they went downstairs. He touched in his card at the counter. The girl at the back of the shop was still singing quietly, absorbed in her work.

'I'll come back soon.'

'Please do,' she said simply.

'I think I'm going to read real books from now on,' he joked. 'Forget my screen.' It sounded like a pathetic rebellion as soon as he said it, and he felt embarrassed.

Julie just smiled broadly and nodded, and Alec felt that that smile completely accepted him. It was disconcerting. He went off down the street, holding the slightly dusty book.

It took him a while to find his way home.

*

The next day, he found himself suffering from a slight headache and wondered what had made him wander off into the Underclass Area. Nobody he knew would have done that:

it was considered too dangerous. He tried to put it out of his mind, and was relieved to get back to the Info, and to turn his mind to Summergreed, now only a few weeks away. There were already decorations, and special lights up in the square outside U-Chooz Plenty, which he could see from the drinks dispenser in his corridor. There were even some fir trees, he noticed, though it was the summer festival, and the fir trees were usually reserved for Wintergreed.

But then, as the festival week relentlessly approached, there came a message on his home-screen, and he realised that he had unconsciously been waiting for this message ever since he had exchanged glances with the man in the Chestnut bar. He wondered why it was written as a U-mail message, not a U-Vid. It read:

My name's Brian Goodrich. I saw you in the wine bar and I'm sure we were both at the same school? Would you like to meet for a drink? Suggest The Chestnut 6 p.m. tomorrow (Wednesday).

Now this was really odd, organising a meeting face to face. The man might be a complete stranger with some ulterior motive. If he had something to say, why didn't he say it onscreen, like everybody else? But Alec was intrigued despite himself, and he knew he would go.

Wednesday was a routine day at the Info, yet Alec felt a growing anticipation all afternoon. He wondered if it was just the fear of a face-to-face meeting with someone he hadn't got to know first onscreen. He tried to remember who this man might have been at school. Between eleven and eighteen, Alec had been to Viney Hall, a very expensive private Academy which his father had paid for. His father had disappeared when

Alec was only five, but according to his mother, he had come from a rich family who had made their fortune in the financial world, and enough money had been found to pay for Alec's private education. In time the school, and his father, had given Alec the qualifications to be able to go on to university too. But how did this Brian Goodrich fit in? He might be a little older than him, he guessed. Had there been a prefect by that name? He couldn't remember one. He felt increasingly nervous as the time approached for him to leave work.

Just after five-thirty he left the Info and, with the rain lashing down, he ran across the square to the Chestnut. That morning had been fine, so he had left his apartment without an umbrella, and he was soaked by the time he arrived at the bar. Brushing down his jacket with his hands, he picked up an applejooz and went to sit in the window where he usually sat, checked his messages, and looked out into the square, watching the ads through the rain. The wide puddles on the flagstones in the square shone with multi-coloured reflections, shattered and pitted by sharp raindrops. Just after six, Brian came in, folding a large umbrella advertising U-Katz Fashion, collected a glass of white wine, and came straight over to him.

'I'd been hoping for an opportunity to talk with you,' he said. 'I'm Brian Goodrich. I wondered why you'd never been part of our Oldboyz network. Realised I should get in touch personally.'

'Alec Arne,' said Alec, shaking the other's hand nervously. 'Did we know each other at school?' He noticed now that the man was wearing a hugely expensive suit and a thick gold wedding ring. He moved with the relaxed air of the extremely wealthy.

'And at university. Or rather, I was very aware of you. We both read History. And when you came up, you won the poetry prize I'd won in my first year.'

Alec was aware that the unwritten rules that governed most of society didn't seem to apply to the Superrich. They seemed to be much more at ease meeting each other personally, in clubs, playing golf, or in conferences or seminars. While middle-ranking businessmen did all their business by U-Vid, and most people avoided contact with strangers, those at the very top were more relaxed about meeting face to face, on exclusive estates, or in hotels, connecting by private jets. Only they could afford the necessary security. Alec had an intuition that Brian belonged to this class. But what would he get out of meeting Alec in a wine bar? Surely he wouldn't be meeting without some networking advantage in mind?

Brian went on: 'I was a school prefect when you were a junior – and then I was still at Magdalen when you came up to Merton. You were reckoned to be one of the brightest of the new scholarship intake. I wondered why we lost touch.'

There was something odd about all this, Alec thought. He had more time to glance at Brian's face. Brian was looking at him in sympathetic enquiry. His face seemed powerful, but kind. There didn't seem to be any hint of deviousness about him.

'No, I suppose I should have joined the Oldboyz,' Alec said, 'but things happened…'

He hesitated, and then changed the subject. 'How have you been doing?'

'Nothing very interesting. Joined a start-up, made some money, now I work for U-Chooz Innercore.'

He said all this in a casual, self-deprecating way, but he was obviously a high-flyer, because he wasn't wearing a smart-badge. Alec determined to choozle his career when he got home, and wondered why he hadn't done so already.

'Nothing like that for me, I'm afraid.'

'Why not? You were gifted enough.'

'I didn't get a first.'

'Nor did I in the end,' said Brian, laughing for the first time. 'Firsts are only for academics.' As he laughed, Alec was noticing that Brian wore a pair of U-Glasses on a gold chain around his neck, which jiggled about a little on his square powerful chest. Now the man was leaning forward, genuinely interested.

'What do *you* do now?'

Alec felt embarrassed, conscious of his badge. 'If you really want to know, I've been in the Info most of my life. Only middle-grade. But I enjoy it.'

'Weren't you ambitious at all?'

Alec hesitated for a moment, and then found himself saying, despite himself, 'It was when my wife left. I was married too young, you see, while I was still at university. I don't know whether you remember her at all. Katherine Standing? At Jesus? She was my contemporary.'

'Oh yes.' Brian was vague, seeming to have no opinion about her.

'She was very bright and very beautiful. I thought she knew everyone.'

'Oh yes, I do remember something...'

'Now *she* was fiercely ambitious. Ambitious for me too. I wasn't really pushy enough for her. And she resented having a family so early after she got her degree, I think, whereas for me…' Alec stopped. He wondered why he was opening up so much to this sympathetic man.

'How many children did you have?' asked Brian quietly.

'Just one – a daughter. Alice. But she, I mean Katherine…' he shrugged helplessly. He didn't know how to go on.

Brian searched for a new question. 'Are you still in touch with her?'

'No; Katherine went off years ago – took my daughter and left.'

There was a silence.

'You must miss them.'

'Not my wife, no. I loved her, and she was very beautiful, but I came to see we weren't right for each other. I came to terms with it.'

'But your daughter?'

'Yes – I miss her.'

'Do you not see her at all?'

'No, I don't.'

Suddenly, Alec's face seemed to fall away, he lost all control of it, and he put his hands over his face and dropped his head. His shoulders kept convulsing and the tears flowed. He was deeply embarrassed. It was the sort of thing people shared publicly on camera with a circle of screen Frendz, or on a reality show, but not in reality itself, not one to one with an almost complete stranger.

He finally got out: 'She was my future.'

There was a sympathetic hand on his arm. Brian was saying, 'I'm sorry. I shouldn't have been asking you such personal questions. Forgive me.'

After a while, Alec pulled himself together, and glanced around. The two girls with shopping bags were back at their usual table. This time they were talking to each other, comparing something obscene about their boyfriends on their screens, and laughing. They didn't seem to have noticed him. He started to make excuses, pretended to check his messages, and rose to leave, but Brian stopped him with a firm hand on his arm.

'Look, tell me if I'm intruding, but can't you trace her somehow?'

Alec determined to control himself. 'I tried for years. I've an appeal posted, but she'd have to want to get in touch herself.'

'Mmm…' Brian was deep in thought. 'Look,' he said at last. 'It's not really the way to do things, but as you probably realise, I have a little influence in certain circles, who I think could help you with this.'

As Alec sat down again, almost disbelieving, Brian said: 'I don't make any promises, mind, but I'll do what I can.' He then abruptly changed the subject.

They talked a little more of school, and university, and mutual acquaintances; and then, abruptly, Brian took a leather-bound notebook from his pocket, tore out a page, and placed it on the table. He took an expensive old-fashioned ballpoint from his pocket, and wrote on the scrap of paper, and pushed it over to Alec. It had numbers and letters on it, and seemed to be a password.

'Don't put this on your screen.'

'Why not?'

Brian only smiled. Then he said, 'It's a private link.'

Alec had heard of private links. They were used by the Superrich. They offered privileged access to certain people and networks that most ordinary people could never reach. Alec folded the paper carefully and put it in the back pocket of his trousers, as Brian went on: 'In case you ever need to get in touch. Don't use it lightly. Only in extremis.'

'Thank you,' Alec said. It all felt a little strange.

Brian got up to go, and shook Alec's hand. It was almost as if the handshake committed Alec to a conspiracy.

'We'll meet again soon, I'm sure,' said Brian lightly.

And something in Alec's mind found itself completing the sentence: … *in the place where the screens are silent.*

But Brian had taken his umbrella, and was hurrying off into the rain.

*

On home-screen that night, Alec choozled Brian. After studying law at Oxford he had taken a further degree in Beijing, had learnt several Chinese languages, started a business there, been bought out by another, risen to be CEO, and it seemed he was now working for U-Chooz Innercore 'with considerable responsibility in Europe'. It didn't give details of his position here, but working for U-Chooz Innercore, in almost any senior capacity, as a junior director or senior executive or whatever, was to have joined the elite ranks of the corporation with the largest share of the world's richest and most powerful people. There was still a majority of men rather than women, and there were still more Chinese and Indians than Americans or Europeans, but that it was the world's most powerful global corporation was beyond question. How Brian's exalted position would help Alec contact his daughter, Alec couldn't begin to imagine, but he had no doubt it was possible.

Several days passed. He was certain that Brian would contact him again soon, but he had no idea how long it would take. He tried not to think about it, and concentrated on his work. He found Simon particularly irritating at this time, sending overenthusiastic messages about Summergreed, and even trying to get into conversation at the drinks dispenser. Alec sensed he might be rather lonely, as if his U-Frendz were not enough for him.

Alec found himself thinking occasionally about Julie's bookshop, and the little room she sometimes let above the shop. It was stupid, but there was a small part of him that still entertained a fantasy of giving up his apartment and his job, and going to live in a shop in the Underclass Area and help sell unsellable books. It was an absurd idea, of course, but he couldn't help it crossing his mind.

But more importantly, he was still trying to decide what to buy for Summergreed, and was agonisingly undecided. He would stare at the red teddy bear propped up beside his home-screen, and trawl through the ads, but nothing seemed to appeal to him that was expensive enough, even though so many of the products and experiences were angled towards 'the person who has everything'. Whatever you bought, it never seemed to be enough.

Then, only a few days before the start of Summergreed, the event occurred which he had always known could change his life forever.

CHAPTER 4

HE WAS WALKING FROM THE TUBE to the Info one morning on his way to work. It was a hot day, almost oppressive, with the sense that the clouds were darkening and one of those frequent summer storms might be on its way. It was of course impossible to turn your hand-screen off completely – Frendz might need to know where you were – but he had turned it down, as he sometimes did when he was on the tube, and when he turned it up again, he found a young girl had left a U-Vid for him. She looked about sixteen or seventeen, with short dark hair and intelligent eyes, perhaps a little narrower than he remembered them. She wore a fashionable red headband.

'I'm told you're my father,' she said almost indifferently. 'Say hello?' and there was a contact number.

He found his heart was beating fast. He forced himself to walk on and sat on one of the benches in the square. He composed himself to contact the number. This could well be his daughter. She looked the right age and surely had her mother's eyes.

His hands were shaking as he made contact. Her face came up onscreen again.

'Hello,' he said, and then found himself speechless. There was a long pause. She seemed to be assessing him.

'Hi,' she said at last.

He forced himself to speak. 'Can we meet?'

'What do you call this?'

He hesitated.

'What, face to face?' she said at last. 'I heard you were a screwbrain.' He saw a hint of her mother's scorn in her eyes, but perhaps a hint of humour too.

'It would be nice,' he said, lamely.

There was a pause. Alec was struggling with this.

At last she relented. 'Oh all right. Let's say tomorrow night.'

'Where?'

She pulled her face into a strange shape, while she thought. 'Do you know U-Zone?'

'No.'

'On Park Street. It's near you. Screen it.'

'What time then?'

She seemed not to care. 'Say, six o'clock?'

He was about to agree when she said, 'See you then' cheerily and faded from the screen.

Alec sat stunned for a few minutes. He hardly noticed when a large raindrop landed on the bench beside him, and another tapped him on the shoulder. So this was his daughter. After all these years. The one he had read to when she was three. He pictured himself reading *The Gruffalo*.

As he walked over to his work at the Info, he was hardly aware of the heavily falling rain.

He had seen his daughter.

*

The next day, he worked from home, and stopped work earlier than usual. His screen guided him to Park Street, where he arrived at U-Zone far too early, his copy of *The Gruffalo* in his hand. It was a joozbar by day, but judging from the ads in the window it was a conventional orgybar late-night. Franchise owners were encouraged to diversify, of course. As it happened the bar was empty of customers.

He pulled himself an applejooz and sat in the window. The bar was in a respectable suburban street, almost opposite the gates of the park. The evening sun shone warmly on the yellow sides of the cameras mounted on either side of the gates. He wondered if his daughter lived anywhere nearby, and from which direction she would come. The sky was blue today after the rain, though it was still hot and close. Drones passed like birds in the sky. He watched idly a small swarm of mosquitos buzzing outside the window. Occasionally a large one would land on the windowpane.

He was alone in the bar. Apart from the monitors in the ceiling of course, which turned towards him from time to time, as if to check how much he had drunk of his juice, and whether it was time to suggest a refill.

At last, about fifteen minutes late, he saw his daughter approaching along the street from the west; looking very grown-up, he thought, as she listened intently to some music on earpiece. She paused, and flicked the hair from her eyes, before coming into the bar. She pulled herself a juice, and then came over to Alec. As he started to rise, wondering if he should embrace her or shake her hand, she had already sat down in the seat opposite.

'Alice,' he said. And then, 'How are things?'

'Fine,' she said, noncommittally, taking her earpieces out so she could talk. But she held on to them, and twiddled them in her hand, as if she wanted to put them back as soon as possible.

'Is it all right for you to meet me?' he asked, tentatively.

'Why not?'

'I just meant, does your mother know you're here?'

'Er... no.'

'I wondered. Won't she be angry?'

'Too bad. She doesn't rule my life.'

Alec couldn't help himself: he came out with the next question without thinking first. He said, 'What has she said about me?'

Alice smiled. 'It's not very nice.'

'In what way?'

'She says you've got no hard drive.'

'What?'

'Dated software.'

'What does she mean?'

'She means your speeds are too slow.' She was spelling it out now, as if explaining to an idiot. 'You don't measure. No ambition to succeed.'

Alec felt his anger rise. 'How does she know what my ambitions are? She hasn't seen me for years.'

'I'm not here to crash on Mum.'

Alec hastily controlled himself. 'No, nor am I.'

There was an awkward pause.

'I'm glad you got in touch,' he said.

She shrugged. 'Curious, I suppose.'

He glanced up, but she wasn't looking at him, but at the earpieces in her hand.

'I've wanted to see you too. Do you remember me at all? From when you were little?'

'Not much.'

'I used to tell you stories. There was one about the monsters who turned out nice after all. Do you remember?'

She looked indifferent. But he had such a vivid memory of her, perched on his knee as he sat in the old chair by her bed.

'I used to read to you. You had this book' – and he put *The Gruffalo* on the table. 'You knew it off by heart. Don't you remember?'

She tapped the book with her finger but didn't open it. 'I remember the film. I don't remember you.'

'I think you were just about to read when you and your mother...' He faltered. He didn't want to touch the moment Alice had been taken away. She was looking uncomfortable with this conversation. He tried to generalise it.

'Do you still read books?'

'Physicals?' she said. 'What's the point?'

Alec felt suddenly hopeless. He started again.

'Do you know what you're planning to do with your life?'

His daughter seemed to brighten up.

'I'm going to uni first. Probably Oxford. We can afford that. Then I haven't decided. Whatever works. I'm definitely going to make a fortune.'

'Is that the most important thing for you?'

'I want to be Superrich. You can't do anything without money. I'm already working in the holidays.'

'Oh? What are you doing?'

'I'm doing a bit of modelling. Good money. One blink and I'll be on the ads.'

'What, like the girl on the escalators?'

'Which one's that?'

'You know, the one with the hair over one eye who turns and looks at you.'

'Oh, I've worked with her. She's one of my Frendz. We're thinking of going shopping together for Summergreed. She's not as pretty as they make her look.'

'No, I don't suppose so.'

'I'm going to be just as famous as her. Success is just a click away.' She looked utterly sure of herself.

'I wish you luck.' It came out sounding a bit more cynical than he intended, so he added, 'No, I mean it.'

There was another silence. One of the cameras at the Park Gates turned to look through the window at them.

It was Alice who spoke first.

'And what do *you* do now?'

'Oh, I work at the Info. Nothing special. Monitoring.'

She wrinkled up her nose. 'Don't you want more?'

He shrugged. 'I've got enough, I think.' Out of the corner of his eye, he was aware that the camera high in the corner of the room was turning towards him.

His daughter was looking at him blankly.

'Uh?' It was just a questioning noise.

'I sometimes think we could all do with less... stuff.'

It was a counter-thought, of course, brought on by his worries about Summergreed. He felt he was digging a hole for himself.

She looked at him as if he was mad, and then she said, 'Do you often think stupid things?'

'Probably.'

And then she came out with the old cliché, but with an oblique sense of humour: 'Need a feeling, need a call,' and spoke to her hand-screen. 'Amber?' It was a moment before Amber came up onscreen. 'Hi, I'm just around the corner. I'll be with you in five.' And to Alec, 'Must go.'

'Can we meet again?'

'Why not?'

She got up from the table and moved away. When she reached the café door, she stopped and turned her head slowly towards him. It could almost have been the girl in the ad, but with dark hair. She asked, as if trying to work him out, 'Do you have a girlfriend?'

'No.'

'Orgybars?'

'No.'

She was disbelieving. 'Sex-booths?'

There was a pause.

'Are you celibate then?'

'I suppose so,' he said.

She laughed, and then shrugged.

'It's a choice.' And then, after a moment –

'Oh… Dad,' she said in disgust, and left.

She called me 'Dad', he thought. He hardly noticed the ping of the 'Payment Taken' as he left the café in a state of euphoria and some confusion. He hardly noticed a bicycle swerve as he crossed the road into the park. The two yellow cameras on the gate swivelled to follow him as he walked off down the path. He had no idea where he was going, till he became aware of sitting by a pond on a bench some time later, staring at the water, and the mosquitos flitting over its surface.

He had made contact with his daughter. It was amazing, but so strange. Over the past years, he had gone over and over his memories of her in his head, but they were all memories of early childhood, of walks with the pushchair, playing with Lego, trying to follow what she was saying. Of course she wasn't interested in that now, in being a child, learning to read, it would be just embarrassing to her. Now she was a teenager, neither a child, nor yet really an adult. Of course she would be interested now in celebrity and money and success like all teenagers of her background. He couldn't blame her. And presumably she had been brought up by the pushiest of mums. She had given away nothing about her life at home. He hadn't asked if her mother had a new boyfriend. Did she think of Alec as her real father? His thoughts raced round in circles. But surely now they had broken the ice, they could meet again. He would at least get to know her better. If he had never been able to be a father to her till now, he could make up for it in the future, could perhaps help her in some way, contribute to her life, make up for the lost years. Perhaps he could achieve some intimacy in his life after all.

He became aware of a movement in a large beech hedge on the far side of the pond. He could hear the soft rustle of a bird's wings in the depth of the hedge. Alec became certain a bird had a nest there, a family. Slowly a thrush emerged, flew up and perched for a moment on a branch of a nearby tree. Then it raised its head, spread its wings and poured forth an exquisite torrent of song. It seemed to Alec to broadcast such a message of hope and joy. It was not the bird's freedom he took delight in; after all the bird had no choice, as he had, and it is choice that makes us free. But he could feel its joyous bond with its family, its fierce desire to protect its young, its steady hope to provide for their future. After a while, the bird returned to the beech hedge and dived into it again, thrashing about noisily.

He was half-aware of another movement by the pond. On a tall post, a rusty UCTV camera stirred, as if momentarily distracted by the thrush. But now it settled again to keep its gaze steadily on Alec, quietly providing his security, protecting his future.

We rarely dream in colour, but that night Alec dreamt in the most vibrant colours: of a countryside where he soared on the wings of some mighty multi-coloured bird, over a Green Country dotted with villages, and trees and fields, and felt the most joyous feeling of hope he had ever known.

*

The next day he was in confident mood. He wondered if he should wait for his daughter to contact him, but couldn't resist contacting her first on U-Vid, to ask her when they could meet again. The connection was busy, however, so he left a message: 'Next Saturday, same time?'

In a few moments she replied: 'Of course not. It's Summergreed, stupid. Stuff to get. Saturday after?' He readily agreed. A fortnight – a fortnight's time. He tried to stop his mind fixating on that fact. He must keep control of his expectations or he could ruin everything. He kept telling himself *I must put no pressure on her. I must let her lead her own life, I must be calm, leave it to her to decide how much she wishes to see me.* But he couldn't help the excitement that built in him.

In the few days left before Summergreed, he found himself thinking again about the bookshop in the Underclass Area. He began to wonder if this could be the bookshop where he had once bought the children's books that he had read to Alice when she was a child. The place had seemed so strangely familiar to him, and it would certainly not have seemed so odd to venture into the Underclass Area in search of books, fifteen or twenty years ago. Though he was behindhand with all his personal screenwork, he decided to make a quick expedition at the weekend to see if he could find the bookshop again. He dared not be long away from his screen, because the week-long build-up to Summergreed began on Monday.

He found it difficult, retracing his steps, and lost his way more than once. Eventually he came across the row of shops with the sign *Julie's Bookshop* at the end; but by now he was anxious to get back.

The shop was empty and quiet as ever. At the sound of his coming in, a bell had rung, and shortly Julie could be seen coming up a passageway. There seemed to be a back parlour beyond the shop, and perhaps other rooms he hadn't noticed before.

'It's Alec again,' he said.

'Hello again,' she said, and there was her open smile.

'I wondered if I could revisit your children's section. Just for a moment. I haven't long to spare.'

'Of course.'

She led him upstairs, and he looked quickly through the books as she watched him. The books had similar titles to those he remembered: *The Very Hungry Caterpillar*, *Where the Wild Things Are*. It all seemed familiar, and it was possible he'd chosen books here many years ago, but his memory was so unreliable.

They were in the room at the back with the bed.

'Did you say you rent this room sometimes?' he said. 'How much do you charge?'

She told him.

'That's very reasonable,' he said.

'And there's a yard out the back which you could share if you wanted to.' She indicated the window and he looked out. There was a yard, with some big boxes in which vegetables grew, spinach and tall beanpoles for runner beans, now with a few red and white flowers. In the yard next door, a substantial woman was silently hanging out washing. He looked back at the antique clock and the bed. There was a deeply peaceful, homely feeling to the room. In the other room, at the front, Alec glimpsed the young shopgirl he had seen before, standing on a short ladder, rearranging some books. She was humming happily to herself.

'Is she your daughter?' he asked, and immediately wondered why he'd assumed that. He had daughters on the brain. But the shopgirl was about the right age to be Julie's daughter, and it was not impossible. The girl heard his question and turned towards them.

'In all but name,' said Julie, and a look of happy complicity passed between them, before the girl went back to her bookshelves.

Julie asked, 'Do you have children yourself?'

'Yes, I have a daughter too,' said Alec proudly. 'She's hoping to be a model.'

'She must be beautiful.'

Alec smiled and there was a silence. He was suddenly aware of that almost tangible atmosphere when two people are quietly in some place together alone, without any pressure to talk. She was looking directly at him, her head to one side, with a slightly enigmatic smile. He scratched his thin beard. For a moment he thought he might say he would like to rent the room. But then he took out his screen, remembering all the personal updating he needed to do.

'I'd better get back. I'll come back after Summergreed, when I have more time.'

But really, he thought, it would be impossible to rent this place. It didn't fit at all with the new picture he had of his daughter and the future connection he hoped to have with her. He could not imagine her approving of his spending any time here. He left the shop and hurried home. He must concentrate on the things that really mattered. There was Summergreed Saturday, and then, the following Saturday, he would see his daughter again.

*

And so, at last, it was Summergreed. Saturday was the great opening day, the start of four weeks of excess spending to boost the economy. On Monday, when Alec went to work, he saw that U-Chooz Square was full of extra flags and music. All week, at lunchtime there were exhortations through loudspeakers, and extra ads streamed into people's earpieces. The U-Chooz mascot was a teddy bear and there were fluffy teddy bears everywhere. *You need to spoil yourself,* seemed to be the message; *you are special, you can have anything you want, be anything you choose.* It was a carnival atmosphere, a celebration of the individual, of personal freedom and choice, and it built all week to a crescendo of desire. Then, on Friday, there was the day of fasting, of holding back, of waiting, of delicious anticipation. U-Chooz Plenty was closed all day, the square quiet and deserted.

But on Saturday morning, almost before dawn, the crowds started to gather in the square, waiting for the doors to open at 10 a.m. Coaches were arriving and disgorging their customers in U-Park areas for miles around, and lines of people processed through the streets, converging on the square as if they were on pilgrimage to a holy shrine. Alec travelled in especially to join them. It would have been impossible to resist the celebration. The day was already blisteringly hot, and in many ways it would have been more convenient for everyone to stay at home and order what they wanted onscreen as usual. But inside U-Chooz Plenty, special offers had been prepared, bargains that could only be collected in person and paid for at special counters. At U-Chooz stores all across the country, preparations had been made for the onslaught. It was interesting, Alec thought, as he sat on one of the square's benches, that though every individual was alone with his or her particular dreams of purchase, yet the crowd still behaved as one unit, with gathering excitement as 10 o'clock approached. At five to ten the huge square was packed and a low murmur began to pass around the crowd, a hum of longing which rose into an almost painful rhythmic thrum of desire, a violent drive to possess that needed to be satisfied. The crowd started to build pressure at the doors of U-Chooz Plenty and Alec too rose from his bench and pressed forward, unable to stop himself.

All of a sudden, there was a wild scream, as the great glass doors of the building sprang open. The thick mass of people flowed into U-Chooz, widening out into the space, heading for the sales points, flowing up the silver staircases, gathering like bees around honeyed counters, tearing at clothes and food, fighting each other in the furious urgency of their greed. Alec found himself lifted off the floor and, carried by the density of the crowd around him, he was hurled through the middle of the building, past one counter, then another. All around him were almost sexual moans of pleasure and excitement; screens were raised above the swirl, while people committed to payments and claimed their discounted purchases.

Alec was tall enough to see above the heads of most of those around him, but he was not strong, and found himself battered from side to side, squashed and pulled this way and that, quite unable to get near a counter, in spite of a terrible desire in him to reach some bargain, to book some experience, to buy some trophy that he could carry from the battle. At one point he felt a violent bang in the face, and he briefly saw Simon elbowing his way past him, screaming out with a kind of twisted joy, 'Isn't this hell?' At another point, he was nearly dragged under by an eddy in the crowd surging towards a furniture display, who stamped on him mercilessly. But with the adrenalin pumping through his body, he hardly felt the blows at all. It was impossible to avoid joining in the frenzy. He nearly found himself paying for a 3D printer on special offer, which seemed to be available in the kitchenware department, but he couldn't keep his place in the queue for long enough. Somewhere in the back of his mind he knew he would have no room for it in his flat – though perhaps it could go in place of his coffee machine which he rarely used, and it was such a tempting price, so he fought as hard as he could. A few minutes later he was in another queue, and he had no idea what it was for, but the people around him were so substantial, and had already gathered such huge bags of possessions, that he was nearly suffocated. And still the crowd lusted and pushed and screamed and tried to enter their purchases at the counters before their neighbours could.

Eventually the crowds seemed to thin a little, creating just enough space for violent fights to break out. It was hot and people began to strip off their shirts; around him, Alec noticed couples urgently retiring to the sex booths or to darker corners. Some were now stripping off their trousers and skirts and rolling on the floor in ecstatic release, unable to contain themselves. He saw a man urinating in a corner, plashing over a nearby couple who seemed to take no notice. But even in the excesses of the orgy that developed under the spinning cameras, every individual held their screens tight and their bags of purchases close. It was all one great blur of possession and consumption, and from every corner of U-Chooz rose a great groan of release.

Alec found himself standing still and silent in the middle of the floor, feeling nothing but disgust. This orgy happened twice a year, at Summergreed and Wintergreed; it was quite normal, it had gone on since the dawn of time. The middle ages had their May Days, the ancient Greeks their Dionysian revels, what was so different? He always tried to join in, but for once something in him stopped dead. Perhaps it was only because he'd not been able to buy anything: he'd had no luck at all. He began to back out towards the exit, picking his way carefully through the crowds. It seemed to take a long half-hour. He felt like a surviving soldier, picking his way through a battlefield of dead and wounded. There was a great silence and emptiness in his head.

Finally, he reached the exit gates. Automatically, he reached for his card and fed it into the slot in front of him, and pushed forward. The gates resisted his push; at first he couldn't think why, and pushed again. He sensed a movement in the surveillance cameras high above him, as they swivelled and converged to point down at him. He looked up as an alarm began to sound. He looked down again and came to his senses. He knew now what it was. For the second time in a few months he had bought nothing. It was his recurring nightmare. His card had been swallowed.

This was the Withdrawal.

CHAPTER 5

AND YET, A MOMENT LATER, the gates released him after all, and he tumbled out into the blinding sunshine of the square. For a second, he felt an irrational surge of relief. He had not been arrested by security. He was still a free man. He crossed the square, feeling shaky, to sit on his favourite bench.

But it didn't take long for him to reflect that his card had been withdrawn. He could do nothing without his card. He couldn't go home, he would not be allowed on the tube. He could conceivably walk home, though it would take him half the night. But if he got there, he couldn't get through the gates of his estate, let alone into his apartment block. He couldn't get into his office at the Info…

He looked back at the huge doors of U-Chooz Plenty above which was the proud motto *Choice Makes You Free*. But he hadn't chosen anything and had lost his freedom. He was trembling all over.

The midday sun presently seemed unbearably hot on the top of his head, and he walked over to find the shade of the Info. There he took out his screen. He might be panicking unnecessarily. Surely the Retrieval Office would be open at all hours, perhaps especially on the opening Saturday of Summergreed. All he would have to do would be to go back into U-Chooz Plenty. There must be a Retrieval Office somewhere in that vast building. This is not my morbid dream, he thought. Don't panic, trust your screen.

But his screen was not just turned down, it was off. Completely black. Card and screen, of course, were inextricably connected. The dark, empty face of the screen in his hand was terrifying, like a foretaste of death. He felt weak in his legs and slipped down the wall of the Info, until he was sitting on the paving stones, full of foreboding, still staring at the blank screen. He started to talk to it, asked for his daughter. It remained inert. He tried one or two of his U-Frendz. Nothing. Frantically he tapped the screen, and began to ask for every number he had ever memorised, but there was no response. He felt sick.

Then, quite suddenly, the screen brightened of its own accord, and a face appeared. It declared cheerfully: 'To recover your identity, you may now proceed to the Office of Retrieval, Room 7107 on the 71st floor of U-Chooz Plenty.' It was a recorded message.

Alec almost ran across the square and back into U-Chooz. He took the lifts to the right of the entrance, but they only went as far as the top of Retail on the 30th floor, and without tapping in a card, he couldn't use the lifts to go any further. He was forced to use the stairs.

It was a long climb to the 71st floor and he had to stop several times. Sometimes he would pass others as he climbed; sometimes he would be passed by others when he stopped. He assumed they were all similar unfortunates, all heavily sweating as they climbed, all avoiding eye contact in their shame. He sensed a woman with pearls, expensively dressed; a man in overalls.

His legs were aching when he finally reached the 71st floor, and came to the Retrieval Office. There was a large outer waiting room, with several other distressed customers, waiting to be called to one of the inner rooms. Everyone had to register their arrival on a keypad. Alec pressed Option 3 to meet a personal advisor. In this situation he would prefer to answer to a human being. No one spoke, no one had a working screen, everyone sat with bowed heads. Alec must have been there for an hour or more, while those before him came and went. He sat in a steel chair, staring at the carpet worn thin by the feet of penitents before him, his mind as blank as his screen.

Eventually a voice announced: 'Alec Arne. Please proceed to Room 9.'

He went in. It wasn't a big room: functional, a wide desk with quite a pleasant-looking woman behind her screen, and a chair in front for him to sit on. The woman was dressed in the yellow U-Chooz uniform worn by corporate therapists. She indicated for him to sit, and looked at him for quite a long time in silence, as if taking in everything about him. All the information, knowledge and experience seemed to drain out of him and into her, until he felt like a small child. Eventually he decided to speak.

'Can I have my card back please?'

It was as if he was asking for the return of a ball, which he'd knocked over the garden fence by mistake.

'I'm afraid it's not quite as simple as that,' she replied, in a soft, reassuring voice.

'What do I have to do?'

'By the way, Alec, I'm Mrs Xian. But you may call me Annie-May. We value the personal touch. I hope we'll both have a really positive experience.'

'Thank you, Annie-May,' he said. 'What do I have to do?'

'We've looked at your spending patterns, your clickstream. We don't jump to conclusions, but we felt we needed to check you out personally.'

'Yes, of course,' said Alec, still feeling like a child. 'I do similar work myself at the Info.'

Annie-May smiled pleasantly. 'Of course you do, Alec. We all have to check on each other these days,' and she laughed lightly, showing her excellent teeth, which had probably been whitened recently.

There was a pause.

'Perhaps you'd like to tell us your problem, Alec?'

There was a long pause. He wondered if she was qualified, as a psychologist or therapist. Eventually he replied.

'I've been worried about the future.'

'What you really mean is you're worried about your daughter.' She smiled and went on, 'Do you think you'll worry less, now you've seen her?'

Alec thought. 'Oh yes, I'm sure I will.'

'And you'll start to enjoy life, Alec. You'll contact your U-Frendz more.'

'Oh yes, and I'll spend more.'

'You'll be more involved with your screen.'

'If you'll let me.'

'You'll accept your online responsibilities.'

'Yes, I will.'

'Good. That's very satisfactory, Alec.'

'May I have my card back now?'

'I'm afraid it's not quite as simple as that,' she replied in a soft, reassuring voice.

The repetition was unnerving, and there was another pause. Alec felt he should say something. But in the end Annie-May spoke.

'You see, you seem to have reservations, Alec.'

'About what?'

She shrugged. 'Spending. Growth. Advertising. Technology. The war.'

'How do you know what I think?'

She just smiled. Alec knew from his own work how easy it was to infer thoughts from people's behaviour. But though he might have had a few strange counter-thoughts, he hadn't been conscious of Resistance in any real sense.

'We've been watching the patterns. It's not just your obsession with your daughter. The negatives here are quite suggestive. You've shown very little enthusiasm to join the rest of us, and your social credit scores are sinking. And yet you have your personal screen, the advertising is tailored to suit you personally, U-Frendz are your personal friends, the spending is entirely for your benefit, the war is for your safety. We are thinking entirely about what suits you as an individual human being; what reservations can you have?'

There was a silence.

'Perhaps you'd like to tell us your problem, Alec?'

Alec had no idea how he should answer. He just needed to get his card back.

'I'm sorry,' he said at last. 'I'm sorry I'm not as good as some people. It's just that I...' He stopped. For some inexplicable reason he seemed to be watching Katherine carrying his baby over the brow of the hill. He felt the tears starting up.

'That's right, cry if you want to. It's all good. It's natural.'

'I'm sorry, I should want to think more about myself.'

Now another memory flashed through Alec's mind. He was only a child. It was Easter in the old days, and his mother was suggesting he share a chocolate egg with his sister. He snatched it for himself, and ran away to hide it under the stairs. When he saw his mother again, it was as if nothing had happened. *I got away with that*, he felt; *she doesn't mind if I'm selfish and greedy.* But perhaps she was only teaching him the proper way to survive in life, the only way to behave. The sad thing was that, by the time he'd next looked under the stairs, the chocolate was twisted and hard and stale.

'I'm sorry,' he found himself saying. 'I'm really sorry. Can I have my card back?'

'I'm afraid it's not quite as simple as that,' she replied in a soft, reassuring voice; and it was then that he realised he wasn't talking to a real human being at all, but to a kind of projected hologram or animated reconstruction. She looked solid enough. He was probably also in a virtually constructed room, but he couldn't be sure. He looked around, trying to spot the joins.

Annie-May seemed to have hardened a little, as if she realised he had seen through her persona.

'I see tears like yours every day, and anger; though there's very little point in getting emotional with me...' She considered a moment. 'Let's start again. You're intelligent, so let me be quite open with you. We are beginning to understand how the embryo of dissent may develop. We distinguish between Economic Resistants and Political Resistants and understand better now how these distinctions should be dealt with. And, to be frank, we're a little worried about your life and background, so we must ask you a few questions, before we can decide to which category you belong, and what course of action to take.'

All the emotion had drained away from Alec, and he felt cold and alert. But he knew if he were truthful he should have nothing to fear.

'Now,' she asked, 'why do you think your wife left you?'

'Katherine?' Alec was taken aback by the directness of the personal question. Then he said, 'I think she was frustrated because of the baby. She felt it was slowing down her career. She wanted to be rich and successful and felt the baby was holding her back. We used to have rows about it, terrible rows.'

One such row came to his mind. He could see Katherine's distorted face as she flung a child's plastic plate at him across the kitchen.

Annie-May looked doubtful. 'But if she was so frustrated by the baby, why did she take the baby with her?'

Alec felt trapped by this question. 'I don't know,' he said at last.

'She must have loved the child more than you did, or she would have left the baby behind.'

'I think it was to spite me.'

'Really?'

'She knew how much I loved Alice.' In his memory, Alice was hitting him over the head with a pillow, over and over again, and each time he was pretending to cry. Alice was helpless with laughter.

'The truth is, you didn't want to spend money on the baby.'

'We didn't have much money. And I didn't want to spoil her.'

'Why is buying things for the baby spoiling her? You could have bought her some expensive toys. Wouldn't it have been showing how much you loved her?'

'I suppose so, yes.'

'So perhaps you didn't love her enough?'

Alec found himself speechless. Finally he said, 'I bought her books.'

'Only because you didn't want her to get too close to her screen.'

'I don't remember.'

'You wanted to deprive her of the closest relationship of her life. Were you jealous of her screen?'

'I don't know.'

'Perhaps the real reason your wife left you was that she was frustrated, not by the child, but by you.'

'Well, yes. She would say I wasn't ambitious enough, that I'd never amount to anything. But I was working, working very hard. I was looking after Alice.'

'But Katherine was providing all the money for the family.'

'I tried to help. That's why I joined the Info.'

'Only part time. And who looked after Alice when you were working?'

'Well, of course, we relied on underclass help then.'

'Which Katherine paid for.'

'I admit it. But she earned so much more than I did.'

'Exactly. Which is why she left you.'

After a moment's silence, Annie-May resumed: 'Why didn't you shop online for a new partner?'

'I didn't want to make myself vulnerable again.'

Annie-May was now referring to the screen on her desk, though Alec was certain all this knowledge about his background was already stored inside her holographic brain.

'After Katherine left,' she continued, 'you had a sort of breakdown.'

'Yes I did.'

'You just stopped going to work. We have your hospital record... psychiatric care... and then you just took off. The suggestion is that before you left you became obsessed with your background, your DNA?'

'Yes, I went to find out my roots.'

'Very fashionable once.' Was there a hint of a sneer?

'I just wanted to understand myself better.'

'Of course. So you left our system for... about a year?'

'About that.'

'Where did you go?'

'I went East.'

'We know. How did you spend that year?'

'I went to visit family, travelled. Is there anything wrong with that?'

'Of course not. In the twentieth century many people went East to find themselves. But this is the middle of the twenty-first. And these are dangerous places now. What concerns us most is that there is a gap in your record.'

'I know. It was a difficult time for me.'

'Go on.'

'I prefer to keep it private.'

'Private?' Annie-May seemed appalled, but Alec found a sudden streak of stubbornness.

'It's my personal choice.'

'Privacy is not a choice.'

'It's my individual choice.'

'Do you think so? I think you'll find individual choice is about the positive satisfaction you get from the things you openly choose to buy, the Frendz you openly choose to like, the online interests you openly choose to follow. Privacy is not a choice, you don't make a positive choice to be private; it's better described as a withdrawal.'

'Withdrawal?'

'It's the opposite of choice. Choice is freedom. Privacy is a restrictive cage, it leads to isolation and resistance. It's a withdrawal from life.'

'Withdrawal...'

'And if you withdraw from us, then we will withdraw from you.'

Alec went cold.

'But I try to join in as much as I can,' he said. 'I got confused just now at the gates, but I tried to buy lots of things, I work hard, I try to keep up with everything, but there's so much to do online, and I...' Alec felt he was pleading now, and was disgusted with himself.

'It's the way it all adds up. You've been wandering about the Underclass Area. You've made undesirable contacts online, said you could do with less stuff. You've even looked up the Caliph. Listened to terrorist propaganda…'

'No, that was because –'

'You're quite free to do as you like, of course, but you can see there are definite hints of Resistance here, both political and economic. It all raises questions.'

'How am I to manage without my card?'

'Your card was issued by U-Chooz. It's a privilege, not a right.'

'How will I live?' Alec was beginning to panic. He was to have met his daughter again next Saturday. What was to happen now?

It was as if she read his thoughts, and she smiled again, showing off her whitened teeth.

'I think you need to volunteer for Re-education, don't you?'

'If it helps,' he said, feeling helpless.

She seemed to relax a little now. 'I'm glad you freely chose that option. Don't worry, we'll make sure you're looked after. We don't think your case will prove too difficult, so it shouldn't take long. Your Frendz will be informed. And then, when everything is resolved satisfactorily, you can carry on with your life at the Info as if all this had never happened.'

'Really?' said Alec hopefully. He felt almost grateful.

'As we all know, the innocent have nothing to fear. Now, is there anything else we can do for you today?' She seemed to be about to conclude the interview.

'Is there nothing I can do to appeal against this?'

'Oh, of course. We live in a free country, you are allowed to make a videocall before you begin. So who would you like that to be? It's your choice.'

Alec thought quickly. A solicitor perhaps, but he hadn't needed a solicitor for years, since he and Katherine had separated and he'd bought his own apartment. With all the legal knowledge online, it seemed possible such people didn't even exist any more. One of his Frendz? But he couldn't imagine any of his online Frendz making a special effort to help him, not even Cally from the Diggers, who had disappeared in any case. He could already feel the shame of his re-education bouncing about the web. He thought of his daughter, but what could she do? Perhaps one day she might want to help him, but she could have no loyalty to him yet: he had only just found her. And then he remembered Brian, the man who had the power to find his daughter, who had shown so much sympathy for the difficulties of his life. And he seemed to be simply the most powerful man he could think of. This was surely an emergency.

He took the scrap of paper from his back pocket, with Brian's passcode on it, and read it out to Annie-May. He had some satisfaction in saying, 'It's a private link.'

Annie-May stared. She was absolutely still, as if in a state of shock, almost as if she'd heard personally from the CEO of U-Chooz. Or perhaps she had been paused.

She began to say, 'We value every customer personally,' but her voice faded and her image dimmed. Then the whole room went dark.

Alec sat for a while, confused and frightened. Then he rose and tried to grope his way back to the door by which he had entered. He found it and turned the handle, but it was locked. He moved about for a little in the dark. It seemed he was trapped in a small black cube of a room, empty apart from the one chair he had been sitting in. In despair, with no idea what to do, he sat down in it.

Instantly the wall beside him lit up, and there was Brian's reassuring face, filling the whole wall.

'Don't worry about a thing, old fellow. I'm sending my driver to collect you.'

CHAPTER 6

TWENTY MINUTES LATER, Alec was sitting in the back of a luxury limousine, speeding smoothly through London on dedicated U-Chooz lanes. It was a long time since he had been in a car. The traffic seemed to consist mostly of luxury cars or U-Chooz vans and lorries. On the inside lane, there were cabs that appeared to be driverless, but his car had a chauffeur.

Alec tried to talk to the driver, who had been silent.

'Where are we going?'

'You'll see.'

Alec sat back and tried to enjoy the deep leather seats. But he felt uneasy. He had checked his hand-screen, and it was still blank, refusing to respond, and his card had not been returned to him. It must still be somewhere in U-Chooz Plenty or the Retrieval Office, and every mile was taking him further away from it. He wondered if Brian truly had the power to issue him with a new one, or bring his screen to life.

Now he was on a motorway. He assumed this was the old M4, but he couldn't be certain. He tried to memorise where he was going. He noticed where they drove off the motorway; and very soon after, he was driven up a laurel drive to a big country house. There was a massive front door framed by a portico with white pillars.

The chauffeur opened the door for him and let him into the house.

'Take off your shoes,' said the chauffeur. Alec left his shoes by the front door. The man led him across a hallway, up the curve of some deep-pile carpeted stairs, across a landing, and into a large study. The room was dominated by a wide desk, and there were great plate-glass windows looking out over a parkland vista of ancient oaks.

Behind the desk sat Brian Goodrich, working at his screen. He rose at once.

'My dear fellow, I hear you've had a bit of a shock.'

'Well, yes.'

'Come and sit down. Take off your badge and relax. I'll ask Rafiq to bring some coffee. Or would you prefer tea?'

They sat opposite each other on sofas, while a Syrian servant brought coffee on a tray with an antique silver coffee-pot and fine china cups. The sofas were real leather, and as luxurious as the car seats. Though there were framed artworks on the walls, the eye was drawn away to the spectacular trees in the parkland outside. The whole room was carpeted in a pale soft pile, and Alec enjoyed the velvety sensation of the carpet, warm under his socks.

'I'm glad you got in touch. Couldn't let an old boy get dragged into the machine without a murmur,' said Brian, smiling. 'I had to find out what's going on. You must tell me all about it.'

'I'll try,' said Alec. He couldn't help noticing the big wall-screen behind Brian's desk, which, though turned low, was humming slightly.

'Is that bothering you?' said Brian, rising. 'Shall I turn it off?'

'Can you do that?' asked Alec, stunned.

'Of course,' said Brian, and smoothly turned towards the screen.

The screen spoke first. 'Shall I give you twenty minutes?'

'Thank you. That should be fine,' said Brian and the screen turned itself off.

Brian settled down again on the sofa opposite, and there was a deep silence. There was normally a very slight hum from the screen, and Alec realised what a persistent presence that hum was in the background of his life. It was strange to feel the silence as he and Brian looked at each other. He was reminded of his dream. *We shall meet where the screens are silent.*

'Do you want to speak first, or shall I?' said Brian with a slight smile.

'I don't know. They've withdrawn my card. My screen is dark. They think I'm a Resistant in some way.'

'And are you?' He said it lightly, as if it didn't matter much.

Alec hesitated. He wasn't sure what he was.

'Don't be shy. It's a free society. You can say whatever you like, especially here. Nobody's going to judge you. You could say… well… you could say "Fuck U-Chooz" if you like, no one cares.' He laughed almost merrily. Alec found himself laughing too, slightly amazed that Brian seemed to have mirrored a thought that he had almost had himself a few weeks ago.

'Fuck U-Chooz,' he tried out, echoing Brian. But it sounded rather more nervous and unsure when he said it, which made them both laugh.

'Not a very sophisticated thought, but it's a start,' said Brian. 'How about... Stop Economic Growth!' This he cried out quite suddenly, and it sounded so odd it made them laugh again.

'Stop the war!' rejoined Alec, and there was more laughter.

'Join the Resistants!'

'Hurrah for the Caliph!'

Soon they were both laughing so much, the tears ran down their faces. It was absurd but Alec felt a great sense of release from all the counter-thoughts that had been oppressing him.

'You know, the one thing I loved about Oxford were the conversations,' said Brian when they had calmed down somewhat. 'Did you find that? You could sit up half the night and discuss politics and art and how to reshape society and anything you wanted. Great times, weren't they? Lucky, privileged times.'

'But then...' ventured Alec.

'Oh yes, then there was the real world. But doesn't it just prepare you well – thinking everything through.'

'Yes, I suppose it does.'

'Hey, did you know I've written a book? Well, I don't know if you could call it a book exactly – probably won't be issued on U-Books. More for myself and to circulate among a few friends.'

It was strange, but Alec could almost physically feel the spelling – that Brian was saying friends and not Frendz.

'I'd really like you to look at it,' Brian went on. 'Even just the introduction. I'd like to know what you think.'

'Of course I will – I'd like to,' said Alec warmly. But after a moment: 'This card withdrawal… what can I do? I don't even know how I can get into my apartment, or get back to my screen for work.'

Brian looked thoughtful. 'You know what, I think you should stay here tonight. I've got to go off for a face-to-face tomorrow, a U-20 economic forum meeting in Shanghai. I shan't be back for a week or so. But I could use the time after supper tonight to look into your case, and try to sort it out before I leave. If all goes well, my chauffeur can take you back to your place tomorrow. How about that?'

'That's great,' said Alec, and felt a flood of gratitude, and almost reverence for his new friend. How kind of him, he thought, how kind.

'I'll talk to the screen later tonight. But first, let's have something to eat. Rafiq!' He called the servant. 'Let's have a spot of supper in here, if you don't mind.'

'Of course. I'll talk to the cook,' said Rafiq, and went off towards what Alec presumed were the kitchens. At that moment, the screen that had been silent behind Brian dimly came to life again.

Over supper they talked about their school and different teachers, and university societies and May Day punting on the Cherwell, and they drank a bottle of excellent wine together. Alec found himself avoiding the subject of Katherine, because he didn't want to betray his emotions again, though he couldn't help wondering about Brian's private life. He wore a wedding ring, but if he was still married, where was his wife in this huge mansion? He found himself skirting round the subject. Perhaps his wife was away at present, or more likely

83

they too were separated, and he lived alone. Few people stayed married for any length of time.

At one point he asked: 'How long have you lived here?'

'About ten years. I lived for a while in Brighton. I've always loved the sea, but I needed to come back to London. Partly personal reasons, but partly to be nearer the airport. The trouble is, I'm needed so much abroad.'

Alec was impressed. Flying was mainly for the rich. Certainly the underclass never travelled for holidays abroad, as they had once done.

Suddenly he felt horribly tired. Brian sensed it. 'Look, you've had a terrible day,' he said, and went to a drawer in his desk. 'Here's this book I was going on about.' Alec was surprised to see it was in the form of a bound script. 'Take it to your room. Rafiq will show you where you're sleeping, and you can have a look at the introduction at any rate. Or you may prefer to leave it to the morning, and we can talk a little then. See what you think. I'll try to find out about your case in the meantime. What do you say?'

Alec was thankful, took the script and, saying goodnight, followed Rafiq to his appointed bedroom. It was a luxury en-suite with a huge bed and another view over parkland. A pair of pyjamas lay on the bed. In the bathroom were all the things he needed.

He went to stand at the window. The fresh summer-green trees in the park, oaks and chestnuts, were swaying slightly in a brisk wind. The sun was beginning to set and could be seen flashing through the side-branches of a massive chestnut tree, so that flickering patterns of light and shade were cast into the room. There was not a drone to be seen here, though the sky was crossed with a few broad vapour-trails, and starting to turn a darker orange between the trees. After the claustrophobia of the city, he felt a flicker of hope, a sense that life could be more open and free.

Closing the curtains, he changed and climbed into the luxurious bed. He felt awake now, and curiously exhilarated. There was a screen on the wall of course, but it was only dimly alive and he could see no other cameras. He felt comfortable. He decided to read a little, and opened Brian's book.

*

INTRODUCTION

Almost from the beginning of recorded time, there have been three kinds of people in the world: the Elite, the Middleclass and the Underclass. The Elite have always been obsessed by the preservation of their position; the Middleclass have aspired to become the Elite; and the Underclass have merely suffered and survived as best they could.

Elites traditionally tried to preserve their power by hereditary means, aristocracies passing their power from father to son; but the Elites that lasted longest turned out to be those where the institution remained constant, while the personnel remained open to change, as in the Roman Catholic Church. In the first half of the twentieth century, new Elites of this kind, both Fascist and Communist, pursued power with a single-minded lust unrivalled in history. Stalin, Hitler and Mao pursued the cult of power for its own sake, expressed best in the image of 'a boot stamping on a human face for ever'. They ruled by a cult of personality, and by propaganda provoking mutual suspicion between citizens at home, and promoting nationalistic fervour abroad. But the pursuit of pure power eventually became unsustainable, because it relied entirely on fear to keep the rest of society in thrall. After the fall of the Berlin Wall in 1989, these tyrannies mostly collapsed, though a few clung on, or briefly surfaced from time to time.

The new elites, which came to replace those based on fear, emerged from the liberal free-market system which eventually spread throughout the world, from the West to China, and led to the first truly 'globalised' elite.

The genius of this elite is to realise that there is not one, but two great drivers of human nature: not only fear, which is negative, but greed which is positive; and that previous elites failed because they concentrated only on fear, and neglected greed.

Of course elites had always tried to control the other classes by raising their standard of living just enough to buy their loyalty. But now a more systematic approach was employed. The problem of overproduction, which had been solved in the twentieth century wholly by war, was now solved primarily by encouraging consumption. Consumerism had to be pushed to the point of addiction, because it was understood that the more the masses became obsessed with consuming and acquiring, the less likely they would be to challenge the elite. In spite of occasional economic crises, this system has accelerated into the present world of indulgent plenty. Ever more luxury goods are created, and credit extended, debt created, and money printed, to keep the wheels of growth ever turning. Side effects, such as obesity, resource depletion, waste, pollution, climate change etc, can and must be ignored. This is the true meaning of Control by Greed. It is, if you like, 'stuffing a burger into a human face for ever'.

For the new elite, who probably number less than 10,000 individuals worldwide, power is not the primary aim any longer, though this can be enjoyable. The true end is wealth for its own sake. The salaries, bonuses, shares and acquired assets are more than can ever be spent on their own luxuries. The wealth of the richest is now out of all measurable proportion to that of the rest of mankind.

But for this elite to preserve its power and wealth, let alone to survive and prosper, the lessons of the past must be properly understood.

First: The system must appear to be meritocratic. The underclass can be largely ignored, but the middle classes must always feel they can achieve membership of the elite, if they work hard enough. This is not to say that the elite should not buy every possible advantage for their own children, but in theory it must remain an open system. Which individuals have the money is not important, provided the hierarchy is maintained. Like the old Catholic Church, it's not concerned with perpetuating its blood, but perpetuating itself.

Second: It must remain amorphous and anonymous. The idea of a Big Brother on every screen has proved to be counterproductive, because although it may be a focus for loyalty and love, it can also too easily be a focus for hatred and revolt. If the leaders of U-Chooz are never in public, there is no focus for discontent. It may be argued that a logo or a brand may provide such a focus, but it is not so easy to attack as an identifiable personality known to the public. (Politicians can be a useful distraction here.)

Third: It must remain above the law. In practice this means it must be tied to no country. This can be achieved by the use of tax havens; by the gradual hollowing out of nation states using privatisation; and by ensuring the absence of any international regulations. Leaders of countries who want to join the elite must pass laws and pursue policies to encourage this process further. The result is that U-Chooz, for example, has now a GDP bigger than any government on Earth, even China.

Fourth: It must appear to uphold moral values. The impression must be given that the elite work in the common interest. It follows that greed and wealth must be presented as moral values in themselves. All growth is of value; no distinction can be made between good growth and bad growth. Maximising shareholder 'value' is a moral imperative, irrespective of consequences. The elite upholds green 'values', so any environmental damage, pollution or waste must be 'externalities', and the cost of these borne by the other classes. Nor can any elite individual be held legally or financially responsible when their corporations fail. Fines may be imposed since money is no problem, but never jail sentences. The elite are too valuable. It must be admitted that there are certain paradoxes inherent in these values, and a certain amount of necessary 'doublethink' may be required.

While these lessons from the past are learned, in the meantime all other classes must be encouraged to embrace the idea of Greed, partly by producing and advertising ever more attractive consumer goods and services, partly by encouraging faith in an ever-rising standard of living. Everyone must buy into the system through their pensions and share options. The cycle of desire must be maintained at all costs, if Control by Greed is to be effective.

But the other driver of human nature must not be neglected either: Control by Fear. Here the past can be more positively instructive.

First: The Permanent War. Some way to keep the population of the free world in fear has always been necessary. After1989, an exaggerated fear of Communism was replaced by an exaggerated fear of Islamism; but the utterly self-destructive wars of the twentieth century were no longer necessary. The Permanent War can now be fought from a distance. Though it is good to give the impression that it is our national soldiers who are bravely fighting in defence of democracy, our operations are mostly conducted by proxy, by mercenaries and U-Chooz private security abroad, or by drones from thousands of miles away. The vast majority of casualties are taken by the enemy and mostly go unrecorded; but they provoke suicide bombers at home, and together with vivid reports of casualties and atrocities, they keep the population fearful and angry. It is sometimes asked how a few desperate suicide bombers can really be a force to conquer the world. Here again a certain amount of 'doublethink' may be necessary, and it can only be noted that it generally does seem to work on public opinion.

Second: Surveillance. From cameras in the street, to two-way screens, the ability to control information has grown exponentially in a way that would have made the old dictators drool. From Africa to the Pacific, there is hardly a place left in the world where humans do not connect personally with their screen, whether wristed, handheld, desktop or built-in. All knowledge, decision making and emotional life now flows through the screen, and the involvement between the individual and screen has become the most meaningful of all relationships. Control over this relationship has become a great prize.

It is interesting that, in early years, the internet was considered very much a democratic tool. Dissidents with the ability to hack systems could cause great havoc, and flash mobs could bring down governments, if only temporarily. Governments fought back. But tech corporations were always the greatest collectors of information and quietly superseded governments in the skill with which they developed control over the systems universally in use. Eventually huge banks of servers stored the data on every individual's clickstream and analysed the information, at first selling it on purely to maximise profits, but soon realising it could also be used to control society. While the location of power-grid centres or food-supply warehouses could be discovered, and these were sometimes attacked (e.g. 2024, 2038), the servers that controlled the whole system gradually became more compact, centralised and increasingly secret, till those in the elite who knew about their whereabouts were restricted to a very small number, perhaps a few hundred people worldwide. As governments weakened, and corporate power grew, U-Chooz in particular was able to buy up the best talent, gather the most information, and become increasingly able to weed out or buy up anyone who threatened their powers, who became known as Resistants. We will return to the question of the Resistants in Chapter 7.

The present writer is unequipped to analyse the central workings of the elite at its highest level, but it is generally held in the 'Innercore' that, although quite invisible to the general public, at the very top of the food chain, as at the centre of any web, there probably lies...

Alec stopped reading. He thought he had heard a noise, somewhere in the house. Softly he slipped out of bed, padded to the door and looked out. Down the dark staircase he could see there was a shaft of light shining from a half-open door. He ventured across the landing to the top of the wide stairs. He thought he could hear voices: one of them certainly Brian's, the other a woman's. Alec presumed that Brian was talking to his screen, perhaps asking for information on his case. But then Brian's voice was raised in anger. Strange, he thought, because the screen was always polite and designed never to provoke anger. It was unlikely that Brian would be contacting any real official in the middle of the night. He wondered if this might be Brian's wife, whom he hadn't met yet. Perhaps they would meet over breakfast.

His eye was caught by a movement above him to his right. On the landing ceiling, a camera was turning to look at him. Time to go back to bed, he thought.

As he climbed into the massive bed, the screen on the wall said gently, 'Do you need to know where anything is, outside this room?'

'No thanks,' he said, and settled down to sleep among the downy-soft pillows.

*

He slept dreamlessly for the first time in years, and only woke when he sensed Rafiq standing over him with a breakfast tray. The tray was placed on the bedside table. There was coffee, a freshly boiled egg, toast and marmalade.

'Brian is working in the study, and is happy to be disturbed whenever you're ready,' said Rafiq, and left the room.

Over breakfast in bed, Alec dipped briefly into Chapter 7, to try to find out what 'Resistance' meant. He read:

Resistance to the elite almost never comes from the Underclass. There may be constant gang-warfare, violence, vandalism and lawlessness, but it is generally directed amongst themselves and is no threat to the elite.

Political Resistants are commonly terrorists. They are mostly religious, literalist and extremist supporters of the Caliph, in effect members of a criminal cult. Apart from the occasional terrorist outrage, they are in general sufficiently controlled. Deaths are relatively few in this country compared, say, to road deaths. Nevertheless the impression must be maintained that they are the major threat to our way of life. They must be controlled by Fear, at home and abroad. This involves the police, security soldiers, and secret services.

Economic Resistants can be more difficult to categorise. Largely negative in outlook, they refuse to accept the consumer society, the need for greed, the value of growth, choice, the permanent war or anything else about our free society and are determined to undermine it. Driven by envy, they work in secret, often on the Dark Web, using illegal cryptocurrencies, to resist and restrict the freedoms of the elite. It is hoped that they can be controlled by Greed, can be seduced into conversion, and reassimilated into society. This involves propaganda, targeted advertising, selective Withdrawals, and Re-education.

The two forms of resistance can overlap, and in such cases, both Fear and Greed may need to be employed.

Both forms of resistance have been developing cyber-attacks from the Dark Web, which has become a serious problem in recent years. Several cities have been brought to temporary blackout, and several distribution centres emptied of goods. So far, constant vigilance has ensured that such attacks have only affected the outer edges of society. The inner core of the web remains untouched.

'Did you read my introduction?' asked Brian, when Alec had gone downstairs. He was at his desk, but turned his screen aside when Alec entered the study.

'Most of it,' said Alec. 'It's interesting. I'd never thought of it quite like that.' He wanted to say how radical it sounded, to ask Brian how comfortable he felt in expressing such an analysis. But there were more urgent questions. He stood at the desk, turning his useless screen in his hand. 'Did you find out anything about my case?'

'I'm afraid it's not altogether clear what's going on.' Brian hesitated. 'It was hard to…' He broke off. 'To be absolutely honest with you, there's a bit of an upheaval going on behind the scenes. I can't say too much, but U-Chooz seems to be in rather a state of flux. Some sort of major crisis brewing which is absorbing Innercore discussions. I suspect even my own position may be none too secure.'

'Really?' Alec began. 'I thought –'

Brian raised a hand. 'The less said the better. But it means that right now I'm not in a great place to help you after all. You'll just have to go for Re-education. Don't worry too much, just go along with it. Be open and honest, and I'm sure you'll get your card back and your screen restored without too much trouble. If you're really worried, just give me another call. You've got my link.'

'But how…' Alec lifted his blank screen from his side.

'Any screen will do. You can always reach me.'

'Yes, thank you. You've already been a great help.'

Brian looked preoccupied. There was silence. Alec thought, *something must have happened last night that rattled him.* He didn't like to press it.

'What do I do now?' he asked.

'It doesn't look as if you can go home just yet, but don't worry. My chauffeur will drive you to where you need to go.'

He rose and came out from behind the desk. 'I will be there for you, I won't forget.'

'I can't thank you enough.'

'We old schoolfriends must stick together.'

To his embarrassment, Brian actually embraced him, seemed genuinely moved, almost to tears. He felt confused and turned away to see Rafiq standing at the study door. He carried Alec's shoes in his hand.

As the limousine swung round in the drive, and Alec settled back in his wide leather seat, he glanced back at the mansion he was leaving. He half-expected to see Brian at a window upstairs, waving him goodbye.

And his blood ran cold. There, at the window, he saw the slim figure of a fashionably dressed woman staring down at him. He might have been wrong, he told himself later, because he hadn't seen her for years, but at that moment he could have sworn it was Katherine.

CHAPTER 7

'WHERE ARE WE GOING?'

The chauffeur was silent.

Alec tried to think about what Katherine's presence at the window might mean, but his brain didn't seem to be working properly. What was Brian's connection with her? Had she known Alec was there? Was Brian on his side, or hers? Was Brian betraying him? It was strange, but he found that hard to believe. And yet he was now going for Re-education. What would that mean?

'Where are we going?'

The chauffeur clearly did not intend to answer. Had he orders from Brian? Perhaps it hadn't been Katherine he had seen, but just an image formed by his own fears. But if it was her, what was she doing there? Alec's brain was stuck, going round in circles.

He tried to follow where he was going. They were travelling

west again. It wasn't a long journey. Perhaps it was somewhere near Heathrow.

There was some kind of checkpoint. A man in the dark red U-Chooz uniform seemed to know the chauffeur and waved him through.

'But I haven't got my card, and my screen is dark,' said Alec. 'I even took my badge off back there.'

'Don't worry, everything will be taken care of,' said the chauffeur, speaking at last. He stopped the car, and opened the door for Alec.

There was some kind of an office. A man behind the desk; no windows.

'Don't worry,' the man said. 'Everything will be taken care of. Relax, have a cup of coffee. Do you take sugar?'

Alec felt relieved at this kindness. Soon there was a cup of coffee. It was sweet. Alec's brain was still not working properly. It was almost like a dream. The man watched him carefully.

Suddenly, he felt paranoid. It was urgent to remember Brian's number. He took the paper from his pocket with the password on it and tried to memorise it, in case the paper was taken from him. He tested himself several times until he felt certain he knew it. But the man was still watching him. He put the paper back in his pocket with his screen.

And then he felt distinctly strange.

*

'Welcome to the Hotel,' said a voice.

He woke, and found himself lying on a bed in what appeared to be a hotel room.

His first instinct was to reach for his pocket in a panic. His screen was still there, but the slip of paper had gone and the screen remained unresponsive. He lay still for a moment and tried to remember Brian's number, and was almost certain he had remembered it accurately. He found he was hungry.

He looked around the room. It seemed like a small but standard hotel room: the usual double bed, neutral sandy-coloured carpets, one metal-framed chair. The wide screen on the wall was lit with the words *Welcome to the Hotel*. It felt rather overheated; perhaps the thermostat wasn't working properly. He got up to look out of the window.

He was surprised to see a sandy desert as far as the eye could see. He must have been unconscious a very long time. There were a few tufts of yellow grass, randomly placed; no trees or shrubs. He looked along the line of the horizon, and thought he could just make out rolls of razor wire. There seemed to be nothing else at all. It looked like a very unpromising place for a hotel. He found himself sweating.

There was a brief knock at the door, and a man came in. He was dressed in the standard dark red U-Chooz uniform, and might have been a security soldier. He made no eye contact of course, but was looking at his screen attentively as he said, 'Follow me.' Alec followed him down the corridor to Reception. The soldier was short and substantial, with ginger stubble on the back of his neck.

At Reception, he was asked to wait while a soldier behind the desk checked his identity onscreen. Alec noticed there were other soldiers about, some with guns. The wall-screens were lit mostly with commercials, and the music fed into the lobby was U-Schmooz. One screen showed a map of the Hotel;

Alec went over to look at it and, using his hands, he briefly explored it. It was a large two-storey building with two wings, marked F and G. He couldn't find any areas marked A, B, C, D or E. Perhaps they lay in other buildings, but there didn't seem to be any other buildings for miles around. It was as if the outside world didn't exist.

He walked to the front doors of the building. Nobody stopped him, as a glass panel slid open. The heat outside struck him as intensely as if he had opened an oven door. It was desert as far as the eye could see: no roads, no paths, no drones overhead. He could be in Spain, or Africa, or the Middle East, he had no idea. There was simply nowhere to go, if he had wanted to leave. No wonder no one had stopped him looking out. He stepped back, and the doors closed again.

The man behind the reception desk called him over. He seemed satisfied with his research and smiled.

'Welcome to the Hotel,' he said in excellent English. 'We've had an update on you from Innercore. We're not over-concerned. You'll be glad to hear you're in one of the best rooms in G wing. We hope to make the process as comfortable as possible for you. Customer satisfaction is very important to us.'

'Can you get my screen to work?' said Alec.

'Are you missing it?'

'Very much.'

'That's the right answer!' The man seemed amused.

'And when can I have my card back?'

'In time. The important thing to realise is that all your problems are in your own mind. How long you're here depends entirely on what progress you make. So long as you're not resistant, there's nothing to fear. In fact if you're good, there'll be a lot to enjoy!' He smiled rather suggestively. 'You'll discover it's no fun if you don't join in, but great fun if you do. That's all for now. You'll be introduced to the Program gently. You won't even be interviewed till you're ready for it.'

'Is that all?'

'For now. Oh, and I'd like to reassure you: We Never Use Torture.'

Not altogether relieved, Alec followed the red-haired soldier back to his room. But when the soldier left, Alec heard a click from the door and, when he tested it, he found he had been locked in.

*

He looked round the room. He found that the shelves were filled with clothes, the en-suite bathroom stocked with everything he needed. He was soon streaming with sweat, and decided to shower and put on the new clothes. They were simple: trousers with elastic at the waist and a bright orange U-Shirt, not bad quality, midrange, with the teddy-bear logo on the front. He stuffed his old clothes in a drawer. There was not much air-conditioning, if any, and it still felt very hot. There was a printed card with the times meals would be served in his room. It seemed almost like a normal hotel.

Normal, except that the screens weren't working; only the subliminal hum that told you that you were being watched. There was subliminal music too, electronic mash-ups from past eras, all sounding similar to Alec, with the same regular beat. But it was very quietly played.

The hours passed. Then a meal was delivered by his red-haired soldier. It was a Choozburger and chips, with a Choozacola. He felt quite hungry now and finished it all greedily. After a time, the soldier came and took the plates away. This soldier seemed to have been assigned to him. He tried to involve him in conversation, but the man answered in monosyllables. The longest sentence he could get from him was: 'Can't wait to get home to the kids.'

As the light began to fade outside, small strip lights automatically came on in his room, but nothing else changed. He asked the screen occasional questions, but there was no response, and of course there were no manual controls anywhere.

Another day passed. Meals were the only distraction. He appealed to the soldier to leave the door unlocked, tried to involve him in a conversation about his children, but now the man never spoke, always left quickly, and locked the door behind him. The meals were decent portions of processed food, but he found he wanted more. It was still very warm, and he found himself permanently stripped to his underpants, and taking showers to stop himself sweating.

There was nothing to watch outside the window. In the desert, nothing moved. The only sign of life was the occasional visit of a mosquito to the windowpane, which meant there must be water somewhere, though he couldn't see it. The shadows moved round, but the way his room faced, he couldn't see the sunset. The light faded fast. It was so static in the desert, he almost began to wonder if the outside environment was a virtual world; but inside, the world was certainly solid enough.

He wondered when the Program might begin. He had heard of some brainwashing techniques and imagined he might be starved of food, or they might turn the lights up very bright, or play the music incredibly loud. He tried to steel himself for this possibility.

But then one night the opposite happened. He had just gone to bed when the soft music stopped, and the night lights turned off completely, and he was left in utter darkness, and in a profound silence. After a while it became oppressive. Slowly he realised, for the first time, how much he missed that continuous background of activity on the screen, which had been with him since childhood: the visual and vocal distractions, his U-Frendz, the constant checking of all his connections, even the dim screen, the buzzing in the background, the all-night soft porn. This silence was far more disturbing. Where was he now? He felt utterly rootless. In the night, he even stumbled across to try to open the door, convinced there was light outside, but to no effect.

The next day was even worse. Still there was no life in the screen. Still there was nothing outside but sand, and the thin strip of razor wire in the distance. The time stretched out mercilessly, till he longed to be called in, to be questioned properly, to be accused of something, so he could fight back. He dozed from time to time, and thought of his daughter, of the Saturday meeting, in a few days' time, was it? He went over and over all the things she'd said. He thought about Katherine, and tried to solve the puzzle of whether or not it was her at Brian's house. He tried to rehearse Brian's private link number. But after some hours, that didn't seem to matter; he felt his thoughts become incoherent, his mind going round in circles. Above all, he longed for his screen.

In the third night of almost complete silence, he was woken by a terrible piercing scream, a long scream of agony, and then a voice pleading for mercy, in some unknown language. After a moment, more wild animal screams. He sat up in bed, terrified. He ran to the door, but of course it was locked. The screams were answered by the sound of desert dogs on the perimeter fence; howls almost like wolves. Afterwards, silence again. Slowly he went back to his bed. The screams seemed to have come from a nearby building, but he could not be sure. The phrase came back to him: 'We Never Use Torture'. Then what was this? And who was being tortured?

Another day of deep silence. At some point in the long afternoon, the music came back on, mindless electronic U-Schmooz, and he felt instantly relieved and comforted and grateful. But it only lasted a short while. He had no way of telling how long, because he had no way of knowing the measure of time without a screen. But the music was soon switched off. Back to the silence. And back to the darkness at night.

At some point during the next day, he had no idea when, the wall-screen lit up. It was some U-Chooz compilation. Two toddlers stumbled towards each other, both looking at their screens, and knocked each other out, amid howls of laughter. Even Alec laughed. He watched the screen eagerly. The colours were so bright, the movement so vivid. But after a few moments, it was cut off. Back to the dark screen, and the silence.

A few nights later there were those screams in the night again. Were they his fellow prisoners? The first time he had rushed to the door, his instinct had been to help. But now he felt relieved that, for now at least, it wasn't him. He told himself that perhaps the whole thing was just a fiction, a recording played to frighten him. The screams were fearful, but it was when they stopped that he felt most frightened. The silence, the darkness. He felt himself helpless, growing smaller and smaller, the hollow emptiness of it all swallowing him.

The only anchors in time were the meals that were brought to him during the day. These were increasingly enormous piles of U-Chooz fast food – chicken nuggets and pizzas, curries and burgers and piles of chips – and he found he ate all of it, and drank the cola, though he felt sluggish afterwards. These meals seemed to be growing in size. He tried to do some exercises, but he felt lethargic, lacking in purpose. He wondered vaguely if they were putting something in the food.

It was in the middle of devouring another huge plate of fast food that it occurred to him. The screams had been coming from F wing. He was thankfully in G wing. Fear and Greed, the twin weapons of the ruling elite, according to Brian. Perhaps Brian had foreseen this and had wanted to prepare him. Perhaps Brian had wanted him to resist. But if this wing was the place where the screams were silent, where was Brian? And anyway, Alec didn't want to resist. All he wanted was to get to the point where he could talk to someone in authority. He just wanted to explain his innocence, for his card to be given back, his screen to light up, his life to be given back to him.

Finally, at some untrackable moment, the soldier came and called him for a meeting. He dressed quickly in his trousers and orange U-Shirt and followed the soldier down the corridor to another anonymous room.

The room was cool and air-conditioned. Behind the desk was a substantial man with a beard, who came out from behind it, introduced himself as Rex, and shook his hand firmly as if to reassure him that he was no hologram or robot. He was dressed in the yellow therapy suit and had a thoughtful, intellectual face and slightly wild hair, as if he fancied himself as a philosopher. He went back and sat again, tipping his chair back. He seemed reflective and relaxed, while Alec remained nervously standing. Eventually he spoke.

'What do you think of the silence?'

Alec was taken aback. 'I hate it.'

'Exactly. And the darkness.'

Alec waited, as the man considered.

'You know, in the old days,' he continued, 'before civil-isation, the only noise was natural noise. Like the screams of wild animals in the night. And the only light was natural light. But sometimes at night, even the light of the moon and stars could be cut off by darkness. So they were much closer to the idea of complete darkness, complete silence. Reminds us of the moment when the light of life is in somebody, even though they're in terminal pain, but suddenly the light has gone: they've just stopped. Yes, it reminds us of death.'

Alec felt cold. He wondered where this was leading.

'Throughout the ages, men have struggled to understand that. Monks would meditate, train themselves to face the silence. Rehearse death. But they cheated. They didn't really face it. They filled it with their imaginary friend. They created a God to look after them, an afterlife to comfort them.'

He paused for a moment and his face was sad.

'But now we've learnt better. We may not look at the stars much, but we know more about them. We know we're not the centre of the solar system, or the galaxy; and there are billions of galaxies, and the whole universe is immeasurably old and vast, and this tiny planet is a marginalised speck of dust, utterly insignificant in the great scheme of things. And the evolution of the universe is a blind, wasteful force hurtling to extinction, because all roads lead to death.'

Alec felt there must be an answer to this, but he had no idea what it was.

Then the man's face lit up. It became almost jolly.

'Thank God for our screens, eh?'

Alec waited, and the man went on cheerfully.

'Nobody wants to feel the darkness. It reminds us of death. Why face the silence? So we fill what life we have with music, bright lights, and technology, and films, and Frendz, and shows and shops and sex. We've filled the world with more and more noise and light. And it's all good because it makes us happy. And what is life for if it's not to be happy? And now you can choose more and more things that make you happy. Don't they make you happy? Isn't that the point of it all?'

'Is it?'

'Of course. Individual pleasure. And we provide it through your individual screen.'

'But where does it all lead?'

'Ah, leave the big picture to us. We know what we're doing. All we need is the freedom to operate on your behalf. It's a free society, we all need freedom. It's only when people try to resist, that's when it all goes wrong. That's when you get wars and unhappiness.'

'And what about me?'

'That's always the best question: "What about me?" We think you're making good progress. We don't really think you're a serious case, like some. That's why you're in G wing.

We think you should be encouraged. Your screen will still be disabled, but we're going to issue you with a temporary spending card. Just while you're here. The debt can be added to the Necessary Debt on your real card, when you are returned to society. As I'm sure you will be.'

Rex leant across the table and handed Alec a card, and Alec felt indescribably grateful.

The silence could operate without him. It didn't need him. U-Chooz did. It needed to give him his card back.

*

Over the days that followed, Alec felt almost euphoric. He had expected to be questioned more about his life, about some specific moment when he'd resisted perhaps, or been indiscreet on camera, or hadn't worked hard enough to connect with his Frendz, or about his visit to the East when he'd been younger. He'd expected to have to defend himself more vigorously, though he knew he'd never been seriously resistant. But of course they knew that already. They knew all about him, every moment of his life, every chance counterthought; it was all known, as God had known everything when people believed in Him. It was all stored up in the Cloud, in the servers of U-Chooz. They knew all and they forgave him. He would surely try harder now to conform.

Over the next few days, the lights in his room came on whenever he asked for them. When the music came on, it was for longer, and was louder. When the wall-screen came on, it was for longer, and though he couldn't yet use it for communicating with the outside world, he could still watch films. He found his meals were getting bigger and extra touches were added to them: tomato ketchup, apple pie and cream, ice cream, even chocolate. And he found he was loving it – loving every minute of it.

Then there was the hotel shop; he was able to go with his temporary card and use it to spend what he liked. It was not a big shop, but it had several luxury items, and he knew it was part of the process of rehabilitation. He found himself buying the special razor that Simon had recommended, and enjoyed the luxury of using it to shape his beard. He even saw on display the red rubber teddy bear he had once bought from U-Chooz Plenty. He was amazed to find he no longer thought it repulsive, but quite cute, and he bought it all over again. At first he was escorted to the shop by his monosyllabic soldier, but after a while he was allowed to go on his own. His door was unlocked and he seemed to have the freedom of the hotel, though of course there were several soldiers about. He began to feel almost trusted.

Occasionally he would see other people wandering about the corridors, or would glimpse them through half-open doors. Often he carried his hand-screen even though it was not functional yet, partly as it made him feel more comfortable and partly to avoid making eye contact with anyone. He soon discovered there was a large common-room with a bar, and he started to go there in the evenings for a drink or two. There was only a duty soldier in charge and you just helped yourself as usual, and tapped your card on a pay-pad. There were several small single tables round an open area which could have been used as a dance floor. At the far end of the room, there was another door, opposite the one through which he'd entered. He wondered where it led, but didn't feel curious enough to explore it. He sat by himself, as everybody else did, though there were never many people there. One or two of them had live hand-screens which they studied intently, and Alec felt intensely jealous of them. He held his own dark screen in his hand and longed for it to light up. Torn between the alcohol and the need for a screen, he would finally go back to his room to watch a film.

Once, on the way back, he passed a door which had been left open, and something made him stop. A hugely substantial man was sitting on his bed in his underpants, as Alec often did. His eyes were closed as if he were exhausted, and there was froth at the corner of his mouth. The man reminded him of Simon; or was it just that he'd been recently thinking about him? This man's face was broader. But then the man slowly wiped away the froth from the corner of his mouth with his thumb and forefinger, and Alec knew it really was Simon. A tray of fast food was in front of him, and it was piled higher than Alec had ever seen. And his body was now more than substantial, it flowed generously over his knees and over the bed beside him and down towards the floor. Alec wondered why Simon was here, but he wasn't going to stop to speak to him, and he hurried back to his room.

One day, he was playing a simple game on his wall-screen, shooting at the zombie terrorists, when just after his score came up, his wall-screen announced that it was Saturday night and that it was his privilege to reward himself with a party. It crossed his mind that it was to have been a Saturday when he was supposed to have met his daughter, but though he had lost most of his sense of time, he knew that that particular Saturday must have long since gone. He was surprised to find it didn't seem to matter much any more. The idea of the party was more interesting. He knew what sort of party this was likely to be. In the old days Alec had avoided parties. He knew that the public flaunting of sexuality was generally encouraged, because of the association with spending, with acquisition and possession. And the choices were wider than ever now: sex could be performed solo, or shared in public, or online, with virtual partners or in sex-booths, whatever your orientation; whereas in the past it had been restricted, private and secret. It was generally considered a great step forward that safe virtual sex was gaining popularity over the dangerous real-life kind. But the public commitment to freedom of choice meant that the orgybar was an inevitable part of the mix. And Alec, who had once preferred intimacy, had to admit that a public party might be just what he needed right now.

In the corridor, some coloured lights had been strung up across the ceiling and some raunchy, rhythmic music was being played. Some doors, though not all, had opened and dazed people were slowly emerging. Almost all were in their underpants, though some wore their bright orange U-Shirts. Mostly these were women, though there were fewer of them than men. Almost all were more than substantial, flesh over-flowing their underwear. They followed each other along the corridor till they came to the common room. The chairs and tables had been pushed back. There were balloons tied to the chairs and a revolving multifaceted ball reflecting light in the centre of the room. To give people confidence, there would be no conversation, just loud music and flashing, moving lights. Some went to the bar, Alec among them. It was a free

Choozbooz bar, and a screen behind the bar kept repeating 'You Chooz' and 'Choice is Free'. No one was hosting the event that he could see, though there were a few soldiers standing back against the walls in their dark red uniforms, only dimly to be seen.

People were shy at first, and drank without talking; but the beat was insistent and exciting, and gradually a kind of dancing began. People were dancing in their underpants. Women soon took off their shirts. The music subtly changed, the lights dimmed, and through the little door that Alec had noticed at the far end of the room, one or two extra girls came in and started to dance. Some of them were quite young and pretty. The communal relief was palpable. It suddenly seemed good to have sex with total strangers without any responsibility. Why not? It was like Summergreed, and Wintergreed, and no one was hurt. Alec, drunk, let himself join in.

And at the edge of the piles of writhing bodies, the uniformed security soldiers grinned and took videos on their hand-screens.

*

When it was all over, and the soldiers had escorted their hotel guests, drunk and spent, back to their rooms, Alec slept more deeply than he had slept for weeks.

Over the next days and weeks, his re-education became almost complete. He found himself putting on weight, becoming lethargic, eating too much and drinking whiskey in his room. Part of him wanted to discipline himself, exercise, concentrate on something else, but his mind felt soft. What was so wrong with the world he lived in? It hurt no one. It was true that the underclass suffered sometimes, but was not that partly their own fault, for being self-destructive, and not working hard enough? For himself, he was longing to get back to work at the Info. It was true that once or twice he had a vivid picture of the bookshop and Julie's smile, and a feeling almost like yearning came over him, but it soon passed. He was learning to control his counter-thoughts.

He hoped it would not be long before he would be released into society. He would go back to the Chestnut Bar and order a Choozburger and cola, back to his corridor at the Info, and if he was felled by a sharp pain in the back of the head as he walked along the corridor one day, well, he wouldn't know anything more about it, so what would it matter? He had his card; if only he could get his hand-screen lighting up again, his life would be complete. He wouldn't even need to contact Brian.

Then one Saturday – he had no idea how much later, but he knew it was Saturday because it was party night – he was summoned to Reception.

The man behind the desk smiled.

'We don't see you as a threat any more. We're going to release you. We're going to give you your permanent card back' – he leant across his desk with the card – 'and we're going to give the life back to your screen.'

Alec felt the tears welling in his eyes. 'I'm so grateful.'

'Didn't I tell you there was nothing to worry about! As I said, it's our motto here at G wing: We Never Use Torture. You're free to go; transport can be arranged tomorrow, but tonight the party will be in your honour.'

'Thank you so much.'

The man behind Reception beamed, and the screen in Alec's hand, which had been dark for so long, suddenly lit up.

Alec felt the whiskey-scented tears trickling down his nose. Excited by the life in his screen, he went back down the corridor to his room. He sat on the bed for a while and explored his hand-screen, and the hundreds of messages from his closest U-Frendz, and he felt warm and included. But the music had already begun for the party: there was the thump of bass in the corridor. He decided to save his long-delayed conversation with his hand-screen till later.

Still excited, he went quickly down the corridor to the common room where the party was already under way. As soon as he entered, a voice blared out from the big wall-screen.

'This party is in honour of Alec Arne, who has his card and his screen back today and is free to go. Choice makes you free.'

There was a loud artificial cheer from the screen, though the other partygoers showed only a muted interest. Soon he was only one of the substantial people heaving around the room with lust in their eyes. He noticed with approval that even Simon had made it along the corridor today, a pile of flesh passively in a corner, hardly able to choose, but waiting hopefully for someone to choose him. As the music slowed, and the lights dimmed, there was dancing, and piles of naked bodies, and release and sweat and people blindly groping for each other. Alec looked up as a woman with hardly any teeth slid towards him. Then, promisingly, the door at the far end of the room opened.

The slim, naked figure of a young woman almost fell into the room. Alec would never forget the blank expression on her helpless face, all self-assurance gone.

It was his daughter.

CHAPTER 8

SOMETHING SEEMED TO SNAP inside his brain. He wrenched himself free from a pair of large, sweat-slippery arms, and found himself hurtling towards the exit. He headed instinctively down the corridor towards his room, expecting the soldiers to follow him. Only one soldier stopped taking videos, left his place against the wall, and ran after him, calling. Alec burst into his room, picked up the first heavy object he could find, and as the soldier followed him through the door, he smashed him with the metal chair in the face. The soldier fell back against the door, closing it behind him with the full weight of his fall. Using all his strength, Alec swung at him again with the chair, and then fell on him, punching and kicking wildly. A great gash had opened across the soldier's face, with blood and broken teeth spilling from his split mouth. Alec saw the gun tucked into a holster at his belt, and he took it and pointed it at the soldier, his hand shaking, and he could hardly stop himself from pulling the trigger. But the soldier was unconscious now. Alec instead pointed the gun at the door, expecting other soldiers to follow. But there was only the thump of music from the common room down the corridor. He hesitated.

No one seemed to be coming. He looked at the unconscious soldier, trying to judge how long it would be before he came round. It was the soldier with the red hair. He was wearing a dark red uniform, lightweight. Alec started to tear it off, for a moment thinking he might put it on himself as a disguise. There was a messy moment when the soldier came to and tried to get up, and Alec struggled with him, and smashed his head against the door; but with less conviction now, as he knew the wall-screen was watching him, recording every move. For some reason he then dragged the unconscious man away from the door and tried, unsuccessfully, to stuff him under the bed. Blood was pouring from the soldier's mouth. Alec went to the basin in the en-suite and tried to wash his hands. He was shaking uncontrollably. Without conscious thought he had taken a fatal step he had never meant to take. Had he become a criminal, a Resistant, his fate to be transferred to F wing, to become an anonymous scream in the night?

He dared not go back to the common room to try to get his daughter. He knew it would be suicide. He dressed hurriedly in his own clothes, from the day he had arrived. He would leave behind the soldier, and the soldier's gun: he was too frightened he might use it; he would leave behind his card and screen, which they would only use to trace his position. He was on his own. A terror was on him that he had begun a process that could only end in his death. His only thought was a blind desire to get out of the hotel, to get away as far as possible, before the inevitable end.

He ran out into the corridor, closing the door behind him. Then, without looking, keeping his eyes down, he walked as steadily as he could towards Reception. He could hear the noise of the party behind him. It seemed strange to him that it was still continuing, and that he was still continuing to walk, and that the soldiers were all too engrossed to notice him.

He came into Reception. It was quiet. The soldier at the desk was absorbed in his screen, but looked up briefly and nodded to him. He had, after all, been given the freedom to go. As he reached it, the front door slid open.

Outside, the sand stretched away into the distance, with only a few random tufts of yellow grass. He stood there for a moment, in the heat. He tried to ignore how far that sand would stretch. It would extend far beyond his immediate obstacle, the razor-wire on the horizon. If he really was in Africa or the Middle East, he tried to imagine the long, dangerous journey without money, the classic refugee journey across the sea into Europe. And if he ever arrived home, he would be on the run, a fugitive without identity. But the first step was the crossing of this desert. Though the sun was setting, it was still unbearably hot. At any moment, there would be an alarm behind him, an uproar, as soon as they discovered the soldier in his room.

So he stepped out into the burning sand.

As he walked quickly forward, he felt a sudden sense of disorientation. The view of the desert seemed absolutely identical in every direction. It took him a second or two to realise the truth. The tufts of grass had indeed been randomly placed.

A moment later he burst through the exterior edge of the illusion, and stumbling, fell onto cool, wet concrete.

Alec got up quickly and turned around. The long, low building behind him, the building he had been in, was real enough. Two wings, two storeys, the same shaped windows. But beyond and around it there was no desert: just scrubby fields, a few autumnal trees, and the afternoon sun shining between heavy grey clouds. He could hear the sound of an aeroplane, approaching, descending. He was on wasteland, somewhere near Heathrow perhaps. There was a slight suggestion of soft rain.

Then he heard the sharp, insistent sound of an alarm within the building, and instinctively he ran. Up a short grass embankment, there was a fence. Climbing over the fence, there was a driveway. Up the driveway, a road. When he reached it, he looked back quickly. Soldiers in their dark red uniforms were streaming out of the glass-doored reception area. Someone was shouting instructions. He ran along beside the road as fast as he could till he could hear an old-fashioned drone overhead. He set his course roughly to the East, putting the sun behind him, and skirting round every camera he could see. It was not long before he struck the motorway into London; and, feeling that he was at least out of immediate danger, he started to walk beside it, towards the city in intermittent rain.

And the sense of fear and panic that had possessed him began slowly to give way to a feeling of fury he didn't fully understand, and a strange sense of where he was going.

*

Alec stood on Brian's drive and stared at the great mansion for a long while.

In places the curtains were drawn. Nothing stirred. Perhaps the household were on holiday, or Brian was at a conference. He looked especially at the window where he thought he had seen Katherine months ago, but it was dark inside.

He crunched further up the gravel drive, and arriving at the great front door, he lifted the huge brass knocker. The rap reverberated loudly between the wet walls of the house and drive.

He seemed to wait a long time, his heart beating. He needed to know for certain whether Brian was friend or enemy, how Katherine fitted into the picture, whether he was being helped or sold; but above all, how his daughter had come to be involved.

At last the door was opened. It was Rafiq.

'Alec Arne. I've come to see Brian.'

Rafiq seemed surprised.

'He's very busy at present. I'll ask.'

The servant moved back into the house, and Alec followed without invitation. He didn't trouble to take off his shoes and decided that, whatever happened, he would not be cowed, or take no for an answer. But as he climbed the curved and carpeted staircase and followed Rafiq across the landing, he was also conscious that, after everything that had happened, without card or screen he was especially vulnerable.

In the study with its splendid views from the wide windows over the dark oaks and golden chestnuts, Brian was talking quietly with his screen. The room was the same, apart from a pile of suitcases and large boxes to one side.

Brian looked up from his screen as Rafiq entered the study, and over Rafiq's shoulder, his eyes met Alec's. His face went pale.

'Good Lord, my old friend! I wasn't expecting you.'

'Well, I'm back now.'

'I hardly recognised you.' He rose to shake hands. 'You've put on weight.'

'I've been to Re-education.'

'Well, I'm sorry it took so long.' Brian seemed preoccupied as he went to stand by his desk. 'Look, it's not the best of times…' He indicated the suitcases and boxes. 'Moving out, you see.'

'Where are you going?'

'Wait here. There's something I need to do, then we can talk. Sit down for a moment. We could have some coffee.'

Alec stood by the soft leather sofa he'd sat on the first time he'd been to the house, and waited while Brian left through a door at the far end of the room. He was tempted to follow, but waited. He could hear voices. Was that Rafiq, or was it a woman's voice? After a few minutes, Brian returned.

'Sit down, sit down. Coffee will be here in a moment.'

There was a short silence before Brian went on: 'You know I tried to follow your case, but I couldn't get very far I'm afraid. How was it? All resolved satisfactorily?'

'Not really.' Alec was noncommittal. He was still unsure of his ground, and didn't know which side Brian was on.

'I'm sorry to hear that. I'm told Re-ed isn't that bad, if you go along with it.'

'Who told you that?' Alec couldn't help the bitter edge to his voice.

'Oh, it's generally accepted. But of course I've no personal experience.'

'But I have.'

'I'm sorry. It doesn't sound too good.'

'Oh, they work more on Greed than Fear.'

Brian's face lightened. 'That's good! I'd forgotten I gave you my book to read. I've updated it, written some more. I must show you.' He sat down at his desk, and started to explore his screen. 'I imagine you got your card and screen back then?' he added casually.

'No, I left them behind.'

'Left them!' Brian looked up in shock.

'I left in a bit of a hurry. And now I was hoping you could help me; help me understand a few things for a start. And then –'

'Well, I'm moving, as you can see,' Brian gestured towards the boxes, 'so it might be hard.' He seemed to be considering something. Then he turned to the wall-screen behind him. 'Give us fifteen minutes.'

'Of course,' said the screen, and the soft humming died, leaving that uncanny silence. Brian turned sympathetically to Alec.

'Now, tell me everything that's happened.'

Alec hesitated for a moment, and then decided if he didn't trust Brian, he could trust no one, and had no hope of survival. So he began to tell him the outline of what he had experienced in the Hotel. But he found that when he came to the part about his daughter and the soldier, he became speechless and shaky, and couldn't go on. He was in a strange state, between shame and anger. There was a long silence.

'Listen,' said Brian, abruptly. 'You've trusted me. I'm going to trust you.'

But even as he said it, he leapt from his seat and started to prowl around the room. He went to the door at the far end of the room and closed it, checked his desk-screen, and then went to look out of the window. Alec had never seen him look so nervous.

'Did you say they'd already cleared you for release?'

'Yes, they'd returned my card and screen. But then I left them. I think I panicked.'

'There may be something I can do.'

Brian moved decisively back to his desk, spoke quietly to his desk-screen for a while.

'I'm going to take a risk,' he said to Alec. 'I'm going to put a hold, a block on whatever happened at the Hotel after you got your clearance. Erase a small piece of history. The information will still be held somewhere by the servers of course, no one can stop that, but it won't filter through to influence your life. Next, I'm going to set up this duplicate hand-screen and card. They bypass the usual U-Chooz channels and use the Dark Web. What these will do is open up your flat, your workplace, your finances, all your screens without alerting the authorities to any problems. In effect they will give you your life back.'

'How can you do that?'

'It's a counter-terrorism tool we have now, to disrupt activity on the Dark Web, without disrupting the system. In effect, I'm recruiting you into the Counter-Terrorism network, in spite of the fact that you haven't been properly screened. So you must appreciate I'm taking a risk, and honour that.'

After some time he rose from his desk. He had a hand-screen and a card, which he held in front of Alec.

'Don't use these more than you have to, in case of information leak. But you can use them to buy food, access your flat, and your work; just don't use them for anything out of the ordinary.'

Only then did he hand them over to Alec, who was now sitting on the arm of the sofa, and who stared at the screen. It looked like any normal hand-screen, brightly shining as he turned it on, like an obedient pet. The card had all the usual markings.

'They will leave you under the radar, almost as if you were a Resistant.'

Alec didn't know what to say. He knew that without Brian he would have been as good as dead. Eventually he just said, 'Thank you.'

'We're old schoolfriends,' said Brian. 'I wouldn't be doing this otherwise.' He paused. 'No, that's not quite honest. I wouldn't be giving you this if I wasn't leaving the country. This time, for good.'

'For good?'

Brian was at the window again, staring out thoughtfully at the huge trees in the park, which were losing many of their leaves. It was already dusk, and a light, cold rain was drifting through the branches. Alec knew he must have been away for months.

There was a long pause.

'Yes, I shan't see you again,' said Brian sadly. Alec didn't know if he was sad for himself, or for Alec's fate. 'I hope I've helped you, at least for a while.'

'Where are you going?' Alec asked again.

'We have a little place in the middle of the ocean. Many of U-Chooz Innercore live there. In theory we're all meeting for an international conference, but it's thought unlikely that any of us will ever return.'

'Why not?'

'I know you've been away a long time. But there's a bit of a crisis brewing here. It's something that's affecting screens internationally. Though the screen I've just given you should be all right for a while... The official line is that the problem may be some kind of terrorist virus. Turns the screens dark and silent. So far, only in patches.'

Alec noticed now that the wall-screen behind Brian was humming actively again. It didn't seem to be affected.

Brian half turned to follow Alec's glance.

'But some screens are increasingly unresponsive. That's why we have to leave. Things are moving towards some critical point we don't yet understand. Luckily, some of us have private planes, and we've got a life on the islands that's quite sustainable. Many of us have been preparing for this for years. We've plenty of food sources there and we're taking our servants.' He shrugged. 'Swimming pools, golf courses, great lifestyle in fact.' He looked back from the window, looking slightly guilty. 'I'd offer you a place on the plane, but they're all taken.'

'What do you think is happening then? This critical point –'

'Have you been into the city yet?'

'No, I came straight here.'

'I expect you'll find out.'

'When are you leaving?'

'In a few days. I suppose it's just possible we may come back. Who knows? But I think it's better we should say goodbye for good.'

'I need to ask you something first. About my wife and daughter.'

'Yes?' But Brian had already turned his attention to the boxes and suitcases along the walls.

Alec was about to speak when he heard the sound of a door handle turning from the far end of the room.

'I only hope we've got time to organise it all before we go,' Brian said, indicating the luggage.

'We?' asked Alec.

Brian dropped his voice, guiltily. 'Oh yes, we…'

'You mean you didn't tell him, Brian,' said a woman's voice from the shadow of the doorway. 'You really are a coward.'

Alec remembered the scorn in that voice.

'Darling,' said Brian, heavily, 'you promised to leave this one to me.'

But Katherine ignored him and stepped forward, smiling. She was still slim and beautiful, though her hair was now grey.

'How did you enjoy meeting your daughter, Alec?'

Alec was shocked, unable to reply. Katherine seemed to enjoy his discomfort.

Finally he said, 'Is she safe?' He could hardly hear his own voice.

'Of course she's safe.'

Fury and shame were gathering again in Alec. 'Where is she? What have you done to her?'

'She's here with us.' But, as Alec stepped forward, Katherine went on, 'Well, she's out on a modelling trip today. But she's a happy girl. There's a chance she's going to land a big modelling contract with U-Katz...' Her voice was light, almost indifferent. 'But then again – she might come with us abroad. Who knows? Choice is free.'

Alec was shaking with fury now. 'What have you done to her?'

Katherine smiled, cool and quiet. 'Nothing she didn't choose.'

Without warning, Alec found himself turning away. Just as before, in the Hotel, he didn't think, he just walked, and then ran, straight down the stairs, out of the house and down the drive. Soon he was walking fast in the dark, along the road into the city.

*

He began to wonder why he hadn't stayed longer, to confront her, to challenge her, to find out more. Perhaps I'm afraid, he thought, perhaps I can't face talking to Katherine after all these years, perhaps I can't face a possible truth about my daughter, perhaps I just don't want to know any more.

He couldn't help thinking, she's right if she thinks I am a coward; but it really hadn't been a choice after all, he'd just reacted instinctively: he hadn't chosen to walk out, any more than he'd chosen to strike out at that soldier in the Hotel. Most of the choices we make in life, he thought, don't seem to be rational choices at all. They're not really free, we only wish they were. Even the simplest choices, like buying things, we don't really know what we're doing; only the advertisers know how it works. They pretend that choice is free and rational, because that's how they sell you things. But choice is the opposite of freedom. Choice binds you to your decisions, limits your alternatives. Had his daughter really made a choice to go to the Hotel? Was it possible?

The rain had stopped now, but the wind blew in gusts. He could have taken a U-Cab, but he only wanted to walk and walk till he was exhausted. He watched the road signs pass, one by one.

He began to think, I'm a fool as well as a coward. He had pretended all these years that he had a special relationship with Alice, but it wasn't true. It had been true when she was three, but she was someone different now; he hadn't earned the right to know her, she had been brought up quite differently by her mother. Was she in any real sense his daughter at all? He'd had a completely unrealistic dream about his future and hers. He felt he had finally lost her in his heart. He must come to terms with the grief of that, with the hole at the centre of his being.

All he could feel now was a sudden scalding hatred for Katherine. She had stolen his life, and he had a terrible desire to take a machete to her and split her from head to toe, or point a shotgun to her head and blow it apart, to see her brains splattered across the wall behind her, to see her vacant body drop and the blood flow into the soft pile carpet. But then he had a flashback of the red-haired soldier's split face as he lay on the floor, and he checked himself in horror. What had he already done, in a moment of fear and disgust and panic? To someone he felt no real hatred for. To someone who might have looked forward to seeing his own children that evening. He was not even sure whether or not he had killed him.

He found himself furiously weeping.

He had never seen himself as a violent man; how could he resolve these violent feelings in himself? How could he find peace? How could he ever assuage this terrible fury against Katherine before it destroyed him? How could he ever swallow it, absorb it, without inflicting it on someone else?

It was fully night-time now. There seemed to be hardly any cars or drones going into the city at all, all the traffic was going out of town. Gradually, as he approached the city centre, along the hard shoulder of the motorway, he became aware of a few pedestrians like himself, all going the other way on the other side of the road, sometimes in small groups. Not many people, but a few, shuffling by in the dark. It made him feel slightly insecure.

His thoughts returned to Katherine. He remembered how she had been when they married, how much he had loved her. But he hadn't really known her then, any more than he knew his daughter now. So she and Brian were married presumably. He felt a curious pity for Brian. No doubt the two of them would end up together on some idyllic island in the Pacific somewhere, lounging about in golf clubs, having highbrow conversations in beach bars; no more Choozburgers, just fresh fish and fruit; no more orgies, just tasteful wife-swapping; enjoying the billionaire lifestyle together, while he could go to hell, the whole world could go to hell.

Ahead of him now he could see the lights of the great U-Chooz towers. There was the huge shape of the Hourglass in the night, lit with bright advertising screens at the base, by the windows of the admin offices in the slender waist, and by many squares of light in the looming wider portion at the top, where the financial services lived. There was the squat black form of

Safety in the background, just a crouching shape in the darkness, not lit at all. Alec wondered if people were transferred there from the Hotel, if their cases were difficult. Perhaps only from F wing. And then there was the tall pencil shape of the Info, where he worked.

He was suddenly filled with a great yearning to return to normality, to his work, to the everyday routine of his life. At least this might now be possible. He found himself clutching his new hand-screen in his pocket. There was so much hatred running through him because of Katherine, that all at once it seemed he understood the comforting wisdom of the old slogan: *Beware the person, trust the screen.*

And so at last he approached the city. The familiar slogans were flashing at him everywhere.

CHOICE IS FREEDOM

GREED IS GREAT

ALL GROWTH IS GOOD

And later, when he came to U-Chooz Plenty itself, where the advertisements demanded attention from all sides, and the sign above the doors said…

CHOICE MAKES YOU FREE

… he felt beyond arguing. He felt overweight and unfit, and he had walked for miles. His screen told him it was well after midnight, and he needed to stop.

He tested his card for the first time and went into the Chestnut. It was open twenty-four hours, with card entry, but it was now almost deserted except for one old man in the corner, snoozing over a Choozacola. He was mildly relieved to find his card worked, but he felt beyond thought. He pulled himself an Applejooz. He took off his shoes and rubbed his feet. He wondered idly how long such places would exist. He put his arms on the table and quickly fell asleep.

Opposite him, in the square, the half-naked girl on the bright screen tilted her head suggestively towards nobody at all, and winked.

CHAPTER 9

WOKEN BY THE ARRIVAL OF THE FIRST CUSTOMERS of the day, Alec found himself unusually hungry. He ordered the full U-brek, but then felt too sick to eat it. He couldn't wait till eight-thirty which was the earliest that the Info opened. He found his head was still revolving with the terrible images of his daughter at the Hotel, with flashbacks of the soldier's shattered mouth, with his violent need for revenge on Katherine. But he also badly wanted to be normal again, to prove to the screens and to himself that he was not at heart a Resistant, to repay Brian's faith in him. He needed to test his new identity and personality, to know that it was at one with the old; to be reassured that the trauma in between had really been wiped from the immediate record, forgotten by the servers, to all intents and purposes for ever.

He walked across the square and into the Info. He hesitated at Reception, and felt deeply relieved to hear the ping which told him his identity was accepted there, and he was able to take the lift to the 26th floor. In the corridor he passed some familiar figures, such as Sasha, the girl from a nearby cubicle. Everybody seemed reassuringly normal, avoiding eye contact. They didn't seem to notice he'd been away. He found his familiar desk in his cubicle that he'd left at Summergreed, several months ago. He was strangely comforted by the red rubber bear which he'd forgotten he'd brought into work again, and which was leaning against his screen like an old friend. As he settled in to his seat, his screen lit up encouragingly.

'Hello Alec,' it said. 'You seem to have been away for a while. Welcome back. It's November 9th. Would you like access?'

'Yes please.'

The screen granted it, and he felt such gratitude.

There was, of course, a massive backlog of cases, many of which had been automatically rerouted to other operatives; some had been referred upwards to his shadowy 'supervisors', and a few had been left for him to deal with. The 'Not Very Urgent' cases, he thought. It occurred to him to question how necessary his work had ever been, whether it wasn't part of the huge number of useless jobs created only to keep the economy going. But at least, he thought, he hadn't been cut off during his Re-education. They must always have held out some hopes for him, and he felt encouraged by that. He watched for any of the problems with the screens that Brian had talked of. There was one minor blackout in the middle of the morning, but it auto-corrected almost immediately. Long gone were the days when you had to ask a technician to take over your screen. Now it set itself up again immediately without human help. Perhaps Brian had been exaggerating his worries about the screens, and he and Katherine were thoroughly overreacting, in leaving the country so suddenly. He went back to work, but soon began to feel tired and hungry and decided to take an early lunch.

He went into U-Chooz and bought a sandwich in the concourse upstairs, and some extra fruit in the Food Hall, though he was surprised to find that there didn't seem to be as much choice as usual. He knew he would never again forget to spend there. He unwrapped his lunch on the bench on the square, under a grey sky, and watched the bright advertising screens.

All at once, the lights dimmed on the screens. The few people in the square looked up expectantly. It was a newsflash.

'The terrorist alert has been raised from Orange to Red. The danger is imminent. Please be alert, film anything suspicious, keep your purchases with you. We will update you.'

As usual, there were pictures of soldiers fighting in a desert somewhere, not unlike the desert at the Hotel. A spokesperson then explained that there might be a cyber-attack by terrorists any time now, to take advantage of the economic crisis, but that people must not panic, but try to go about their business as usual. After a while an economic expert from U-Chooz talked about the downturn. Alec watched, fascinated. In his absence he hadn't even been aware there was any downturn. It was explained that it was necessary to make difficult decisions, to do what was right, that U-Bank would print more money to maintain growth at all costs. It was necessary to increase bonuses to the elite, and cut money to the underclass, so as to encourage everybody to work harder to bring back growth. It was necessary to spend more on security to meet the terrorist threat and this would inevitably mean increases in debt. But he finished: 'We must all spend more to save the country we love.'

Alec didn't recognise the speaker, but had the impression that this was an old recording from some previous crisis, being recycled.

The screens abruptly blacked out. They flickered, and went back to the commercials for a moment, but then even the ads seemed to freeze.

Alec waited expectantly. The giant screens in the square had never malfunctioned for more than a second or two in his lifetime. Now they seemed to have frozen, like the flat billboards of history.

About a minute passed. 'What's up?' exclaimed a street-cleaner robot in U-Chooz red, who had stopped a few feet away. A woman crossing the square with a shopping trolley broke into a run.

'I'm going back to work,' said Alec, more to himself than the cleaner, and leaving his lunch for the robot to clear away, started to head back to the Info. He wanted to calm down, to be back at his desk, where he could return to normal.

Near the main doors of the Info, an official crossed his path, staring at his screen.

'Do you know what's happening?' Alec asked boldly.

'Terrorists. Red alert.'

Several people were coming out of the Info tower, as Alec worked his way past them. They were all talking onscreen, sometimes even to each other. Alec walked through Reception, thanks to his new card, and took the lift again, back to the 26th floor. The U-Schmooz music in the lift was comforting.

Somewhere between the 23rd and 24th floor, the music and the lift stopped together, with a squeaking noise and a shudder. Alec was alone in the lift. He waited. This sort of thing seldom, if ever, happened. Was this part of a terrorist cyber-attack? Perhaps, in a moment or two, he would be hurled down the lift shaft and be smashed to death twenty storeys below. The silence grew around him, and he thought of the Hotel. He told himself to be patient, not to panic. He pressed the emergency button, but nothing seemed to happen except the lift said, 'Be patient. Don't panic.' After a while, he sat on the floor, waiting for autocorrect. He studied the hand-screen Brian had given him. It looked like a standard screen, but presumably worked through Dark Web routers. At least that should be working, he thought, and was just about to call for help, when the lift jolted and moved upwards, saying, 'We apologise for any inconvenience. We value every customer personally.'

By the time he reached his desk, the screens were all working, and everything seemed to have returned to normal. At length he settled to his work, but all afternoon he was aware that there were little glitches to the system. He would ask for information on someone, and the screen would tell him 'Information not available', or 'Access denied'. Sometimes this seemed to be on quite routine requests. This sort of thing was rare in his experience, and he was surprised. Was this the result of personal suspicion of him since he'd left the Hotel, or was it the general terrorist alert? The refusals became more widespread as the afternoon went on.

It was towards the end of the day that he walked along the corridor to the drinks dispenser and looked out at the city. The November sky was beginning to darken. Down below, the few great plane trees that remained after the blight a few years ago were shedding their yellow leaves in the dusk, and now the lights were coming on in the great towers.

Then all the lights of the city blinked off, just for a moment, all together, like a giant wink. It was almost subliminal before the lights came on again and Alec doubted whether or not it had really happened. He felt instinctively nervous. There was almost nobody in the building now and the corridor, which might normally be full of departing workers, seemed suddenly deserted. He decided it was time to go home.

He went to the lift, but when he called it, it replied gently: 'Please use the stairs. We apologise for any inconvenience. We value every customer personally.' This did not surprise him, and he even felt somewhat relieved not to risk himself again. He began the long descent by the stairs to the ground floor.

Emerging breathless in the rapidly darkening square, he looked across to U-Chooz, which was normally open twenty-four hours a day in a blaze of light. It was dark, and a surprising number of people were streaming out of the main doors. He set off for the tube station. The public screens were still lit, but motionless, including the ad of the girl which lined the escalators; she was frozen in the act of taking off her bra.

The tube station seemed no busier than usual at this time of day, but he noticed a few people pacing up and down the platform. They seemed particularly nervous. It must be the red alert, Alec thought. On arriving at his home station, he was beginning to feel hungry again, but the local U-Chooz seemed to be closed; all the lights were out. He walked quickly up the hill in the dark, past the Personal Improvement Centre, anxious now to get home. He used his new hand-screen to turn on his home heating in advance.

When he arrived at the iron gates of his home estate, to his surprise the gates were wide open. The main door of his mansion block was also slightly ajar and pushed open quite easily. He wondered if there had been intruders. He went in cautiously, but nothing seemed amiss. At least the door of his apartment was closed, and he was relieved when it recognised his face and opened. He wanted so much for his life to be normal again.

He walked into his living room. It was already warm, and the friendly screen lit up. It spoke softly.

'We've missed you, Alec,' it said. 'Welcome home.'

*

Alec had a lukewarm bath and changed his clothes. Then, as he lay back on his old sofa, Alec realised how tired he felt, how long it was since he'd eaten. He went to the meal dispenser but all the ready meals were rotten and inedible. There must have been some power blackouts while he'd been away, he thought. He relied so much on food being always available that for a moment he wasn't sure what he could do. Send out for a 'luxury' pizza perhaps.

He went to his screen. Gently it prompted him: 'Would you like to check on your Frendz first?' There were hundreds of videos waiting for him. He realised what a long process it would be to catch up with everything. At present his empty stomach was the more pressing need, so he asked for U-Plenty delivery suppliers. As he scrolled the list, he was surprised how many of the luxury suppliers were marked *Business Closed* or worse, *Access Denied*. There were a few names left, and he was in the process of choosing one at random, when his screen abruptly froze, and simultaneously there was an urgent bang on the door. It could only be the blonde woman from across the hallway, he thought, as he went to answer it.

The woman's face seemed even more surgically stretched than he remembered.

'You've been missing,' she said suspiciously. 'Where have you been?'

Alec shrugged.

'I needed help,' she went on. 'My screens went dark again last week. And again just now. I just don't know what to do. I can't work, and I can't get help if my screens are down.'

Alec tried to look sympathetic, as she almost dragged him across the hallway and into her flat. She was in a state of real panic. In the background, possibly in a bedroom, one of the twins was bawling loudly.

'How can I feed them if all the power is down? I can't even order candles, let alone food. What am I supposed to do?'

The lights were still on in the flat, but the screens were dark.

'I don't honestly know,' said Alec.

'I thought you were a techie.'

'I'm not. I only work at the Info, I don't know much at all.'

'But you must know someone.'

'Only through the screens. Have you tried?'

'Of course I have. They just give you standard options: option one, option two. All automatic, there are no human beings to talk to. It's happening everywhere. Is nobody listening?' Her voice was rising in panic. 'One for this, two for that, three for something else. If you do seem to be getting somewhere, it says "Access Denied". Nobody knows anything. It's a nightmare trying to get food. The supermarkets are emptying. I can just about manage during the day, but the nights are so long now. It's getting colder, and the heating just goes off. I press autocorrect, reset, but nothing happens. The nights are becoming intolerable. The darkness and the silence.'

Alec knew about the darkness and the silence. There flashed across his mind the sound of screaming in the night.

'Mum!' came an insistent whine from one of the bedrooms. And then a more urgent order: 'Mum!'

'Stay here!' she told Alec as she rushed away. Alec could hear angry exchanges from the other room.

Alec moved indifferently to the window and looked out at the Underclass Area. It was almost completely dark, just the dim shapes of concrete tower blocks, and eerily quiet.

It occurred to him that he had been trying to recover normality, to carry on with his life as if the world was the same as before he went to the Hotel. But it wasn't. A momentary surge of fury rose up, almost overwhelming him. It didn't matter what was happening to the world, or what became of him now, if he lived or died, it didn't matter, if only he could wreak his revenge on Katherine for what she had done. But the feeling passed almost as soon as it had come.

He found himself still staring out of the window, absently watching a couple of big mosquitos on the other side, part of a small swarm. Their feet were sticky on the windowpane. Bulbous multidirectional eyes stared back through the glass at him. And all at once he realised that they were not mosquitos at all, but tiny drones, watching the room, watching the world.

Outside there was an explosion, and the mosquitos lifted off from the pane and banked away. The cracked walls of several adjacent tower blocks lit up, and there were flames and cries and smoke rising and soon the sound of sirens.

And almost as if he was emerging from a numb state of shock, he made a clear and urgent decision. If there was to be any hope, it lay in the Underclass Area. He must go to the bookshop and, if he could, he must rent that room.

He must find Julie again.

* *

He walked out of his neighbour's flat and back into his own. He saw immediately that his own screens had now gone dark. He went quickly round the apartment turning off all the switches, all the appliances he could find; he had no idea why. Then he packed a small backpack with some clothes, took his winter coat and gloves from the cupboard by the front door, put them on, closed the front door and headed for the stairs.

Out in the streets, there were no street lights. Glancing back down the hill, he saw that the tube station still had a few lights on. The city can't have lost all its lights, he thought, because the sky was still a sickly yellow under the clouds. Important places were bound to have generators of their own. And surely the power would be restored soon. There must be emergency plans for a city as large as this.

Walking as briskly as he could, his bag on his shoulder, he quickly turned into the Underclass Area. He felt instantly insecure. He must try to find his way, in the darkness, to that row of shops with Julie's bookshop in it.

It seemed a long way, a long search. Everything looked different in the dark, every corner, every view of every street. In the tower blocks there were some candles in the windows, and the occasional flashing torch moved about in the darkness.

On one corner, there was a fire blazing in a warehouse. Perhaps this had been caused by the explosion he had heard from the apartments. A few people watched, taking videos.

In another place he heard shouts and screams and down the street he saw a crowd gathering around a food store; it looked like a U-Chooz franchise at the base of an old tower block. The crowd were throwing stones at the windows of the shop, shouting slogans against U-Chooz. Alec could catch the chant 'U-Chooz, You Lose' repeated over and over. He saw the poor franchise owner dragged from his shop, and pushed about by the crowd, before he disappeared from sight. Alec hurried on. He wondered what would happen to the man and why he should suffer the anger of the crowd, when he was only trying to earn a living. But the crowd were now smashing the windows and looting the shop for food. Perhaps the U-Chooz supermarkets were running out of food, and Alec was as hungry as anyone.

He pressed on as best he could in the direction he needed to go. In one street, a large man was running towards Alec carrying a huge cheese and a bag of fruit, including some pineapples. He seemed to think Alec might stop him, and dodged round him, letting out an aggressive roar, while Alec stepped aside.

His legs ached when he arrived at the short row of shops, almost all of which were now boarded up or had their metal shutters down. At the end of the row he could make out the even older shop with a sign over it which he recognised as Julie's bookshop.

It was dark and quiet outside and he hesitated. Then he knocked on the door and retreated into the middle of the road. After a short while, he saw a candle flickering in the upstairs room and a curtain moving, but then nothing. He crossed the road and knocked again, retreating to watch the results.

Suddenly the door opened, and the muzzle of a shotgun pointed towards him. Instinctively he spread his hands wide and said, 'Julie?' He caught a glimpse of her form in the doorway.

'Ah. Alec.' There was a short silence. She had remembered him. He thought he could just make out her smile. 'Have you come to buy a book?'

CHAPTER 10

'COME THROUGH,' SHE SAID, leading Alec through the darkened bookshop and a short passage, where he nearly tripped over some heavy bags. She left the gun in the passage, as he emerged into a back parlour with very old kitchen units along the far side. The room was lit only by the flames from a real fire burning in the grate. He stood amazed.

'Where did you find the wood?' he asked.

'Oh, skips mainly. In your part of town there are so many people wasting wood.' He realised the wood was mostly offcuts of planks and struts and batons from building works.

'It's lovely and warm,' he said. There was a pause, but Alec didn't feel in the least uncomfortable. She didn't seem at all surprised he was there. They both looked at the fire, and their shadows flickered, rising and falling on the wall behind them.

'Please sit down,' she said at last. There was a small sofa and a warm armchair, facing the fire. 'We don't often get visits from people like you! Were you wanting to rent that room?' She was looking at the backpack he was still carrying.

'Yes, if it's still free.' He put down the backpack and sat in the armchair, leaning forward in it. 'I wanted to come earlier, but I couldn't.'

'Why not?' said Julie, with a slight smile, sitting on the sofa.

'It's a long story. I lost my card. They took me off to be Re-educated. I think they thought I might be a Resistant.'

'Aren't you? Everyone I know is,' she said simply. 'But I suppose it must be harder for you, living where you do. They don't bother so much with us, do they? Even when we riot!' There was that smile again in the firelight.

'Is the room taken then?' he asked anxiously.

'Not at all. You can stay here tonight. But we're getting ready to leave, and I've got to lock up the shop before I go.'

Alec's disappointment was obvious. She went on: 'A lot of people are leaving. Everybody's screens are going blank, their power's cut off. We don't have much option.'

'Terrorists,' said Alec.

Julie looked him straight in the eyes and laughed warmly. 'That's what they tell you,' she said, 'but I think it's more serious than that.'

'What is it then? A cyber-attack?'

'They're calling in the debts.'

After a moment, Alec reached for his screen and checked his debt. It was true. There was a notice from U-Bank demanding immediate repayment in full, or there would be denial of service. How could he repay the hundred thousand he'd been encouraged to borrow?

'It's not just people with debts.' She was watching Alec's reaction. 'The man who ran the shop next door saved all his life, now they won't let him withdraw his savings. Everything's frozen. They say it's the crisis and there's no alternative.'

'But how can he manage?'

'He can't. That's why we have to leave. It's dangerous. People are very angry.' But she spoke quietly, without anger herself.

They stayed looking at each other for a moment.

She shrugged and pulled a face. Then she said, 'Would you like some bread and jam?' It must have been the look on his face, because she said, 'Of course you would. Stay there a moment.' She went to the back of the room and started buttering a piece of sliced bread. She put jam on it, put it on a plate, and brought it to him. He ate it hungrily.

She grinned. 'Nobody's going to take it away from you.' It was as if she were talking to a child.

At that moment the young girl Alec had seen working in the shop appeared in the doorway in a dressing gown. 'Can I have some too?' she asked, and waited for Julie to say 'Yes' before she went over to the breadboard in the leaping shadows behind them.

'Did you say this was your daughter?' asked Alec quietly.

'Yes,' said Julie, 'adopted. She was the first child I ever fostered. I think I told you I looked after children.' She pitched her voice gently across the room. 'Come and say hello.'

The girl came over with a plate of bread and jam and sat beside her mother on the sofa.

'And what's your name?' asked Alec politely.

The girl spoke, politely enough too, if she hadn't been speaking through a mouthful of bread and jam.

'Alice,' she said.

*

It had to be a coincidence, Alec thought, but his heart was beating fast and his head was swimming. Alice was not an uncommon name; she might just be another Alice of similar age. He put his head in his hands for a moment.

'You're exhausted. Do you want me to show you to your room?' Julie was saying.

He was standing now, but found himself reeling. He had not realised how hungry and tired he felt. His brain couldn't take any more. He tried to pick up his backpack.

Was it possible he'd got everything wrong? But what about the other Alice? Where had she come from? He couldn't have two daughters. His thoughts were being dragged back to Katherine again, and the flood of violent feelings that were provoked every time he thought of her.

'Please,' Julie was saying. 'Please sit down again.'

He sat. 'I'm sorry,' he said. 'Too many questions. It's just that I have a daughter called Alice as well. She's about your age, and I'm confused by it.'

Julie and Alice looked at each other.

Alec went on, 'And somehow I know you. Have I been here before?'

'I don't know,' said Julie. 'Have you?'

He was at a loss as to how to go on. He wanted them to tell him more about their history, how Alice had spent her childhood, if she had any memories he might recognise. Julie seemed to be reading his thoughts.

'Shall I tell you how I came to adopt her?'

'Please.'

Julie began carefully. 'Well, it was after Mr Charrington stopped supporting the bookshop, and I had to make my own living rather quickly. I started looking after children. Among other jobs, I used to babysit for this rich family.'

'Who were they?'

'Well, I didn't see much of the parents, because they both worked. I just did occasional evenings at first, and then some days, I remember I used to take the child stories – real books I borrowed from the shop.'

'I loved it,' said the girl.

'Like *The Gruffalo*?' asked Alec. 'Or *Bears in the Night*?'

'I don't remember,' said Alice. 'I just loved stories. And I had lots of different babysitters. I just remember I liked Julie best.'

'Anyway,' Julie went on, 'the mother moved away for a while, and I lost contact. But when she got in touch again, she'd split up with her partner and she needed lots of help. It paid well and it became almost a full-time job. I was needed more and more.'

Alec was still thinking, this could be just a coincidence. He didn't dare hope.

Alice seemed a little impatient with the story Julie was telling. 'Anyway, in the end, my real mother decided she was too busy to look after me,' she said flatly, 'and I expect I wasn't easy –'

'That's for sure,' said Julie, raising her eyes to heaven in mock agreement.

'– so she gave me a choice,' Alice went on. 'Did I want to stay with Julie all the time? I didn't mind at all. I never saw my parents anyway. So I said yes.'

'So now we're a family,' said Julie.

Alec felt numb. He knew now what he needed to ask.

'What was your real mother's name?'

'Katherine,' said Alice. 'Why?'

'Because I think I might be your father.'

'We talked about it when you came before,' said Julie, 'and we thought it might just be possible.'

*

They spent the rest of the evening with the firelight between them, making connections.

'I can see you now.' Alec was looking at Alice, remembering her as a baby. He struggled to control his face. 'But I always assumed you were with your mother.'

'She was never there. Always at work. I felt I was in the way mostly.'

'Then why did she take you with her?'

'To Brighton, you mean?' Alice shrugged.

Alec thought, only to spite me. And then for the first time, he wondered if it had something to do with Brian. But he said nothing.

'When I was about nine, my mum's work got so she had to move back to London. That's when Julie came to look after me again. She'd always been my favourite.'

Julie spoke: 'And eventually I was asked if I wanted to adopt her.'

'I was about twelve then. And I couldn't wait to get away.'

'And to be fair, Katherine always supported us generously.'

Alec looked at the worn sofa, the cheap utensils. Not that generously, he thought, compared to what she earned.

'Why didn't we recognise each other before?' asked Alec.

'I was much younger when I first babysat for you,' said Julie, 'and you had so many babysitters. I thought I recognised you when you first came to the shop, but I wasn't sure – you'd grown a beard.' She smiled directly at him. He fingered his beard, which had become ragged again, and was slightly embarrassed.

'And I expect I'm a bit different now I'm grown up,' Alice grinned.

'But I can see you now.'

This time, Alec couldn't control himself and burst into tears. The two women came over to him, and put their arms around him while he cried.

*

At the end of the evening Julie said, 'This is our last night here. We've packed up all our stuff. The power is off, there's no public transport, and the shops are running out of food. Most people seem to think it will get better soon, but we think there may be a bit of a panic if things get worse, so we thought we'd try to get out while we can.'

'Where will you go?' asked Alec.

'I've a brother in the country, and we're going to try to join him. He's got a little place in the woods, near Malvern. We've been talking a lot onscreen, and he keeps inviting us. It's several days' walk to the west.'

'May I walk with you?' asked Alec.

'But you're in a different position, you live in the rich area. Surely –'

'All of the screens are going dark there too.'

'That one's still working,' said Alice, pointing to the screen in Alec's hand.

'So far,' said Alec, 'but I'm not sure for how much longer.' He put it in his pocket. 'And there's nothing for me here.'

Julie and Alice looked at each other.

'You'll have to make yourself useful,' said Julie.

'I'll do my best,' said Alec.

That night Alec lay in the little room upstairs, trying to come to terms. The bed was old but comfortable, high off the floor. The bookshelves on every wall wrapped their books around him comfortingly; and at the end of the bed, he could see where the children's books were kept. Out of the window, the moonlight was shining on the roof-slates of the house opposite. The one screen in the room was completely silent, but the old clock on the mantelpiece was ticking softly. He could just hear the occasional crackle and spit from the settling fire downstairs, and hardly a sound from the streets. It was all utterly peaceful.

And yet he could not stop his thoughts revolving. He was almost certain that this Alice really was his daughter. But then where did all this leave the other Alice? Was that really her name, the girl he had met at U-Zone, that girl at the Hotel? He could see her now as she stumbled through the doorway, her model-perfect face, all self-assurance gone. Was that Katherine's doing? Had she been playing some mind game? Probably. Had Brian agreed to it? Surely not. His thoughts were being dragged back to Katherine again, and the flood of violent feelings that were provoked in him every time he thought of her. She had always accused him of running away, but she was the one who was running now, leaving behind all the devastation, all the unanswered questions. He might have killed an innocent soldier at the Hotel. Why should her life be more valuable than his? She was not innocent, and he felt rage enough to kill her.

But even as the violence swept through him, making his head swim, it was followed by a wave of exhaustion, which seemed to batter him into submission, and he sank into sleep.

He slept for twelve hours or more. When he woke, he found himself looking directly into Julie's eyes. She was crouching by the bed.

'You must wake now. We must go.'

*

At breakfast, they finished the last of the perishable food in the house, and packed up the rest. Julie took an old three-wheeled trailer from the back yard of the house, dragged it through to the front, and all three piled their luggage on it. She took an old-fashioned map from the bookshelves, and then went round the house, checking it was all tidy and secure before they left.

'There's still a chance we may be able to return,' she said, 'when this crisis is sorted out.'

'Hope so,' said Alice.

Last of all, Julie took the shotgun from the passageway, and stuffed a bag of ammunition into one of the cases. She gave the gun to Alec.

'I think you're going to have to carry this,' she said.

'Is that wise?'

'Oh, everyone has a gun of some kind round here,' she smiled, 'and we might need it one day, to hunt for food, or to defend ourselves.'

She locked the front door.

'Goodbye, old bookshop,' said Alice.

They set off on their journey to the west, and now Alec had a gun. His anger hadn't left him.

CHAPTER 11

IT WASN'T LONG BEFORE THEY PASSED the U-Chooz local that Alec had seen looted the night before. It had been burnt out, and was now a smouldering black hole under its concrete tower. There Julie bumped into an old neighbour who assured her that everything would be all right.

'They won't let this go on,' she said. 'They'll sort it all out, and then you'll be sorry you left. I'm staying put, that's for sure.'

But they passed more shops with smashed windows, and looting was going on everywhere. Alec noticed that the presence of their gun deterred people from too much interest in their little cart. They took it in turns to carry the gun or push the trailer.

When they rested, Alec worked out how to use the gun, and made sure that it was loaded and that the safety catch was on.

They passed a crowd gathered round a speaker who was white with anger. 'It's the fault of the immigrants,' he said, 'they're hoarding the food supplies.' They passed a tube station where there was a notice: *All services suspended until further notice.* They passed through a shopping centre where every second shop seemed to be laid waste or on fire. They passed through an area of expensive Georgian houses which looked completely deserted and strangely quiet.

Then, around the corner, there was a massive crowd gathered. A speaker was announcing: 'I know where the Distribution Centre is. We can get food there. Follow me!' People were running to join the crowd as it moved away. There were children screaming with hunger in their mothers' arms, substantial men with angry red faces. Everyone carried a screen, but their screens were dark, mostly unused. The cameras on the corners of the streets were often looking the wrong way, as if they were blind, as if they'd given up all concern for public safety. There were very few artificial lights anywhere; most of the advertisements had died, the screens lifeless. Alec checked his own screen from time to time. It seemed to be one of the few that worked, probably thanks to Brian and the Dark Web. He checked their route through the city.

At one point there were bloodstains on the ground, and some tins of food scattered and also a sleeping bag, which they picked up and added to the trailer. Occasionally they fell in with others, walking the same way.

'Nothing's going to stop me from shopping,' said one woman, laughing, 'card or no card,' before she ran on.

Later they saw some men fighting over a dead screen, which dropped; one of them stamped on it and smashed it, rather than let the other have it.

'Terrible having no screen,' said a bystander, 'like being amputated.'

Sometimes they could hear gunshots in the distance, and once they saw a drone drop out of the sky into a nearby side-street, rolling along and breaking up in a ball of flame.

At length they were walking back along the motorway to the west, pulling the trailer now, on the very path that Alec had taken into the city. There were not many cars passing, perhaps because of a lack of electricity or fuel; but there were more families walking with them now, more and more people on the road, flooding out of the city. It felt safer here, though they could still hear the sound of explosions in the city behind them, and several drones crashed in the fields around them. But they passed some buildings that still seemed to have power, and one sign declaring TOO MUCH IS NOT ENOUGH seemed to be shining as brightly as ever, even in full daylight. When Alec next checked his screen, it told him he was not far now from Brian and Katherine's mansion. And he was aware that the anger was burning in him more strongly than ever.

It was not long before he recognised a particular turning. They had been walking for hours, and he suggested they came off the main road to rest. They turned aside, and found some benches by a small roundabout under some trees, and there they stopped. It was a quiet spot, and seemed safe enough. Brian and Katherine's mansion was probably only ten minutes' walk away.

Alec said: 'Will you be all right here for an hour, till I return?'

'Where are you going?' asked Alice.

'Only to see some people I know who live very close,' he said as lightly as he could, 'just to say goodbye.' He started to move away.

'You won't need the gun,' said Julie.

'I think I might,' said Alec. 'I'll tell you more when I get back.'

Julie and Alice looked at each other. They seemed concerned.

'I promise I won't be more than an hour,' he said, and walked away.

*

As he approached, up the gravel of the long laurel drive, the big house seemed very quiet. The autumn leaves lay in wet piles on either side of the drive. A pale misted sun shone dimly on the brickwork of the huge mansion.

As he banged on the great brass knocker, the front door seemed to give slightly. He waited, but nothing happened. The shotgun seemed heavy in his hands. After a while, he tried the handle of the door, and to his surprise he was able to push it open. He closed it behind him as quietly as he could, and found himself treading over the soft carpets into the house. It felt empty. He went straight up the staircase, towards Brian's study. There, the suitcases and boxes were gone, and most of the pictures, and even some of the curtains. The grand mantelpiece was bare of ornaments. There seemed to be no one at home; they had clearly moved out. The screens were dark, but surprisingly they were still subliminally humming. Perhaps they were kept alive on the Dark Web, or perhaps they were only slowly dying. Alec walked over to the window and stared across the park at the chestnuts, now almost naked. The leaves lay in golden circles round the massive trunks.

He went over to Brian's desk. There he was surprised to see the script of Brian's book, with the pages open at the last chapter. It was almost as if Brian had left it deliberately, knowing Alec would return. For some reason, Alec felt a disappointment that his quarry had gone, and that he might never know the whole truth. There were always so many unanswered questions. He laid the shotgun down across the desk, and picked up Brian's script, deciding he would take it with him.

He was still curious to see the rest of the house, to see again the room where he had slept. But first he went out of the study at the back and discovered a kitchen area. To his surprise there was still good food left untouched in the meal dispenser. They must have private generators, he thought, and had left them on. He saw a U-Katz shopping bag left on a peg, and filled it. This would be a welcome gift for Alice and Julie when he returned. He checked the time on his screen; he still had twenty minutes or so before he needed to start back.

Carrying Brian's script in one hand, and the bag in the other, he went back through the study and found the main staircase of the house. High up on the wall, screens turned at random, and he heard snatches of voice: 'Can I help you?'; 'Do you need to go somewhere?'; but he sensed that their movement was automatic, without meaning or interpretation. Strangely, he felt unwatched. Perhaps it really was possible that the power cuts in the city were not the work of cybercriminals or resistants or terrorists, but because the guiding principle of the surveillance systems had been deliberately withdrawn. The body was still twitching, but the head had ceased to function. Like a decapitated chicken, some of the systems were carrying on mindlessly, though its driving central purpose had gone. Could this really be so?

He came to the bedroom where he had spent the night. It all seemed exactly as he had left it, the soft bed, the pillows, the expensive wall-hangings, the view of the park. He moved on around the house and soon discovered the master bedroom. Presumably this was where Katherine and Brian had slept together. He looked at the huge bed, still made up with its neat white damask counterpane, briefly imagined them making love, and shuddered. There was only one screen here too, and from the wide windows, framed by twisting wisteria, there was an even more spectacular view of the park.

His attention was drawn to the two further rooms beyond their bedroom, an en-suite bathroom and a long dressing-room, presumably Katherine's, with a dressing table and wardrobe. He briefly opened the wardrobe cupboards, and all the dresses were gone now of course, gone with them. Except one dress in the corner, he now noticed, probably one she hadn't wanted to take. And now he noticed there were a few necessary things still sitting on the dressing-room table. A hairbrush, a tube of red lipstick. And just as a strange doubt began to enter his mind, he heard a soft voice from the bedroom door behind him.

'Well, well. Look who's trespassing.'

Katherine held the shotgun in her hand.

*

'The beauty of it is,' she said, 'in law, I'm quite justified in shooting an intruder. Did you come to steal the food?' – she waved the gun in the direction of his bag – 'or was it something else you were after?'

He spoke firmly. 'I want to know about my daughter.'

'Hasn't she grown into a lovely woman? I thought you'd be pleased.'

An image flashed into Alec's mind – a vulnerable body, a frightened face and in the foreground, substantial flesh heaving.

'You had never let me meet her in all those years. Why now?' His voice started shaking.

'I wanted you to know I'd brought her up properly, with the right values. I thought it was about time you saw her, took some responsibility. I did all the hard work.'

'You're lying. You've always been a liar. That girl wasn't my daughter at all, was she?'

Katherine hesitated, and the gun dropped a little. The sardonic smile had gone; she looked almost vulnerable. There was a long pause before she spoke.

'Why do you say that?'

'Because I know.'

Finally she shrugged carelessly. 'All right. No.'

'So what did you do? Hire somebody to impersonate our daughter?' Alec felt almost incredulous, and some of the anger had left him.

There was another pause and then she shrugged. It was nearly an admission.

'Why did you do it?'

She was still trying to look casual, but Alec knew how much she hated to show weakness. He wondered if he might get near enough to take the gun from her, but now she was holding it firmly again in his direction.

She spoke quietly. 'Brian and I talked it over. We knew you wanted to meet your daughter and Brian thought it would be a good idea. But I hadn't been in touch with Alice for years, and didn't want you getting hold of her. So. I spent some time finding the right girl.'

'The right girl?'

'Yes. I wanted to find someone I could be proud of. I wanted you to know that I could hold down a top job and bring up my daughter too. And I wanted my daughter to be ambitious and successful and sassy and strong and everything a daughter ought to be. The sort of girl I would choose to carry on my future.'

'So you hired... a model?' Now Alec was incredulous.

'She was only seventeen. But that girl was going places, I can tell you.'

Alec couldn't find words.

Eventually he said: 'What was wrong with our real daughter?'

'I wasn't proud of her. She was weak and ungrateful.'

'Do you know where she is now?'

'I don't care. She didn't want to stay with me. She left me. She chose someone else.'

'That doesn't sound like weakness to me.'

'She was your daughter. Weak.'

Alec burst out: 'So you forced me to meet the daughter you'd like to have had, in place of your own? What possible reason can you have had for that?' He stopped, and then said, 'Who were you trying to impress? Me?'

There was a silence. To his amazement, Alec saw the tears well into her eyes. For a brief second she looked as vulnerable as she had been when he had first known and loved her. But instantly she raised the shotgun and said, 'You're nothing to me.' There was scorn in her eyes again. 'I'd happily see you dead.'

'Did you know I was going for Re-education?'

'Yes.'

'And did you deliberately send that girl after me?' A moment passed. She made no answer. 'I mean to the Hotel.'

Finally, she said, 'Yes.'

'Why?'

'You needed to accept there is nothing U-Chooz can't make you do. You needed to understand your own weakness. And before you ask, she agreed to go. She was quite happy. So don't get sentimental about her.'

'She wasn't happy.'

'Of course she was. I was paying her a lot of money. She was ambitious. She knew I was a senior executive in the Innercore. She thought I could help her career no end.'

Again, Alec couldn't help the image of the girl's face, and for some reason a flashback of the bleeding face of the soldier, crushed up against the hotel-room door.

'And *will* you help her?' Alec said at last. He took a quiet step towards her.

'I was hoping to. I saw her as part of my future, but I'm not sure I can help her now. The situation's changed.'

Alec took another step towards her, but she raised the gun.

'I could easily shoot you in self-defence. You're in my house.' She was fierce.

Alec decided it was quite possible, and stepped back a little. There was still most of the room between them.

She resumed a more relaxed approach. 'We knew you'd come back. We tracked you on the new screen Brian gave you. I see you've fallen in with the Underclass. Sunk to your own level. Anyway, I thought I'd say a final goodbye before we go.'

'Oh yes,' said Alec, trying to ignore the word 'final'. 'You're off to your island.'

She looked pleased. 'It's the culmination of all our efforts. Brian and I are going to retire there, along with most of the Innercore execs. It's always been the plan. It's just a little earlier than we thought.'

'I expect you understand what's going on here then.'

'Of course we do.' She smiled. 'It's the Withdrawal.'

After a moment she went on: 'Not the petty withdrawal of service from people like you, but the big one.' She seemed to have recovered all her powerful self-confidence. 'It's not terrorists, or some big cyberattack. We're doing it ourselves; U-Chooz are deliberately closing down everybody's cards and screens. All at once. We're withdrawing all food supplies and all services, they're simply too expensive to maintain. It's the logical end to a system that we can't sustain any longer. U-Chooz Plenty, the Info, and Safety are all going dark. A few politicians will be left behind to explain it all in terms of cyber-terrorism. There might need to be some dramatic event as a cover. But what the Withdrawal really means is this. We're withdrawing all the money from all the banks – they're all subsidiaries controlled by U-Bank and the money's ours anyway by law. We've been getting the interest, and now we're calling in the debts and of course we're taking all the savings. And then we're off to the islands. We deserve the reward. We've worked very hard for all this. And now – it's bonus time!' She waved one hand about in mock gaiety; the other hand held the gun.

'But what about everybody else?'

Katherine became more serious. 'We're very sorry for them. They'll just have to fend for themselves. They shouldn't have got so dependent. It's a fundamental principle. People must take responsibility for themselves, face up to the real choices, the hard decisions, what freedom really means. It's only the operation of the market. Survival of the fittest.'

At that moment Alec thought he heard a noise at the other end of the house. Katherine heard it too.

'Is there somebody there?' Alec said.

Katherine backed away, keeping the gun on Alec. Alec followed at a careful distance. When she reached the landing she stopped. They both listened. There was nothing.

'Where's Brian?' ventured Alec.

'He's waiting for me in the car. To be honest,' she dropped her voice to a pretend whisper, 'I don't know how long he's going to be with us. Some of us in the Innercore think there's a possibility he may have been a double agent. Only pretending to do counterterrorist work. They're still considering the evidence. Didn't he try to recruit you?' She posed the question, hoping for an answer, but Alec was silent, and she went on. 'That screen you have in your hand, connected to the Dark Web. Won't be much use to you now, by the way. The Dark Web's closing too. Orders from above.'

'From where?'

'From the U-Chooz servers themselves. They're cutting off all but the most necessary connections with humanity. There won't be many of us left.'

'Why should you survive?'

Here Katherine seemed to shine with inner certainty. 'Oh, we'll survive because we're the most successful, the most talented, the cleverest elite that has ever existed on this planet. We will always survive.'

From where he was standing, Alec couldn't quite see the hallway or the front door, but now he heard Brian's voice.

'Are you coming darling?'

'I won't be a moment.'

'Is that somebody there?'

'That's... Nobody.'

She spoke scornfully. And then she turned back to Alec, trying to look indifferent. 'It's been lovely to talk to you again. I'd quite like to shoot you, but you hardly seem worth it, and I'm just too civilised. You'll probably be dead anyway in a few weeks – not many people will survive the Withdrawal.' She shrugged. 'Everybody's just too dependent on their cards and screens. That's the world we've made, and it seems it's unsustainable. Such a pity...'

She started to move away, and Alec followed cautiously. Carrying the gun, she tripped elegantly down the curved staircase, and across the hall. As he arrived at the head of the stairs, he could see Brian and Katherine standing together at the front door, looking back up at him.

'Happy days,' she said blithely, and left.

Brian lingered for a moment longer, and his eyes were full of sad apology, before he too turned and disappeared through the wide front door.

He had come wanting to kill her; but now it was too late. When he reached the front door, he found the gun leaning against the doorpost and the large black limousine was moving smoothly away down the laurel drive. He put Brian's book into the shopping bag, took the gun and set off quickly; the hour he had given himself had almost gone.

When he arrived at the bench where Julie and Alice were waiting, he saw they were both half-asleep, Alice lying on the bench, Julie propped against their little trailer-cart. Behind them, on the main road between the trees, walked a steady stream of refugees.

*

For a while they walked on with the crowd, in silence, pushing the cart in turns. Occasionally Julie looked at him questioningly but he remained silent, not able to speak yet, to find any words. He would try to tell them everything later.

The people around them were quiet too, and well-behaved, mostly substantial people rolling along with difficulty, some with backpacks, one or two with shopping trolleys filled with their possessions, small children riding on them as best they could. As the afternoon wore on, a few giant mosquitos hung above them, as if shepherding them along as they walked.

Towards evening, when the setting sun was in their eyes, the three of them pulled out of the crowd and stopped on the edge of the road to draw breath. Looking back, a half-moon had already risen, and in the distance there were still some lights coming on in the city, where the great central towers rose.

Suddenly, there was the most terrifying flash of light from the centre of the city, and soon the splitting sound of an explosion expanded and grew into a crunching roar. Everybody in the column on the road stopped and turned. Several miles behind them, the great U-Chooz Plenty tower was dropping, falling into a dense black, billowing cloud of smoke and flame. It fell slowly, bending in the centre, as the bottom of the Hourglass was overwhelmed by smoke on one side and the top of the Hourglass tipped the other way. The violent sound of destruction seemed to go on and on. The setting sun flashed off a succession of windows, as the building twisted and dropped. Then the thin neck of the building seemed to snap apart. The crowd held their breath in awe and amazement as the upper part, which had always seemed top-heavy to the eye, also sank heavily into the smoke below; and a moment later, a new shock-wave of sound reached them, a roaring thunder which seemed to take minutes to dissipate, as the cloud of smoke rose higher and higher into the sky, and spread out till it hid the Safety, enveloped the Info and even darkened the rising moon.

The crowd stood stupefied for a long time. It was hard to take in the destruction of such a building. How could it happen? There were cries of anger and fear; someone burst into tears. Someone said quietly, 'Why didn't we fight back? We left it too late.'

Alec and Julie looked at each other. Alec checked his screen for the first time since he'd left the mansion, and watched the last light fade out of it. Even the Dark Web must have died. And he knew beyond doubt that all the power in the city, all the screens, all the cameras, all the detailed electronic systems that controlled the transport links, the food supplies, the academies, the hospitals, the power in people's homes, it had all been withdrawn.

And as they slowly resumed their journey to the west, he dropped his dead screen by the side of the road.

CHAPTER 12

NOT LONG AFTER DUSK, they made the decision to come off the crowded motorway and take smaller roads into the country. In the hollow of a darkening field, close to a wood, they built a small fire. In Katherine's U-Katz bag they found some salmon marked *U-Chooz Plenty – Green Choice*. They heated it over the fire and shared it. Then Alec told Julie and Alice what had happened at the mansion, just the outline, trying not to talk too much about Katherine. Alice was silent, hardly seeming to react. By moonlight, they retired to the edge of the wood. Julie and Alice shared a small tent, which Alec helped to put up. Then he went into the wood and found some broken branches already gathered into piles, from which he made a primitive shelter against an oak tree. Still fully dressed, he crept under it and tried, as best he could, to get some sleep.

In his half-dreaming state, he thought more about that soldier. The image of his bleeding mouth was always recurring in his mind. Was the man in hospital now, or quite recovered, or had he died? Suppose he'd been brain-damaged? What about his family? He wondered in what Underclass Area he had lived. It was really unfathomable. Alec would never know what he had done, and he would always have to live with the guilt of it.

He also thought about Katherine, how much he'd wanted to kill her and how glad he was now that he hadn't. To his surprise, his great anger had gone. In some ways he felt almost sorry for her now. She would never be happy or content with life on the island. She would find the inertia of retirement boring. He sensed that Brian would end up being scorned, just as he himself had been, and that in spite of all her advantages and untold luxuries, she would still feel somehow short-changed by life. He realised that, though he felt frightened by the unknown future, truly fearful he might not survive, he also felt exhilarated by the challenge; and strangely relieved, just to be leaving the city, and the screens, his work and all the burdens of his old life behind him. From his shelter, he could just make out Julie and Alice sleeping in their tent, holding each other close to keep warm, and he felt glad he had set out on this journey with them. In fact, though it was quite irrational, he felt almost happy.

When the first light began to penetrate the trees, he got up as quietly as he could and went out into the field to the remains of the fire, which was still smouldering. He sat for a moment on a log listening to the first birds beginning to call. In a damp patch, close to the fire, floating on some water, he noticed a couple of dead mosquitos. He went over to look more closely. He picked them up, and after carefully inspecting them, he crushed their tiny metallic bodies underfoot. Then he went over to the trailer to fetch Brian's script from the U-Katz bag. He looked over to where Julie and Alice were fast asleep and then went back to the log and found the page in the book which Brian had left open on his desk for him to look at. He wondered if it was intended as the last chapter of his book, or as a postscript.

By the growing light of dawn, he began to read.

*

THE NEW SITUATION

The elite have realised that the whole system they have devised is no longer sustainable.

The problem is the old one of overproduction. Wars have always been useful here, because bombs are dropped and have to be replaced; countries are destroyed and have to be rebuilt. Consumerism is useful too, because old and obsolete goods have to be replaced, and new false needs have to be provided for. All this enables the system to grow and the elite to become richer. But as the process accelerates into the modern world, weaknesses become apparent.

First: Debt. In the interests of ever-expanding growth, everybody in society has a duty to spend at an accelerating rate. This is only possible by increasing debt (that is, by allowing present pleasure to be paid for by future pain). But increasingly after the sovereign debt crisis, and certainly by the mid 2030s, it was realised that total debts were so large they could never be paid off. The only way left to relieve debt for the elite is to print enormous amounts of free money for themselves so that U-Bank can speculate on derivative 'futures', or so that U-Chooz can buy up the assets of the rest of the economy as it fails. But on all other levels, the debt has become unsustainable.

Second: Resources. In the interests of ever-expanding growth, and supported by subsidies and tax breaks, U-Chooz subsidiaries have established free-market dominance worldwide. When the northern ice-caps melted completely in the '20s, U-Choozenergy moved in for oil. The rainforests were exploited by U-Chooz companies until they disappeared completely in the '30s. The grasslands were exploited for beef, the oceans for fish, rivers for irrigation. But extraction has become increasingly difficult and destructive, and the end product of the whole system is waste and pollution. Many cities such as Shanghai, New Orleans, Osaka and Kolkata are being abandoned because of rising sea levels, and others threatened because of pollution. The feedback loop between exploited resources and global warming has meant that the whole industrial system has become unsustainable.

These problems have long been recognised by the elite. They have known for some considerable time that economic progress has only been possible by creating the 'Necessary Debt'; and by treating the land, water and air as free inputs or 'externalities' that are 'off balance sheet' and do not have to be paid for. Now it is admitted in the Innercore that U-Chooz private profits have only been possible at the expense of the public commons, and it is accepted that this model is now unsustainable.

The question is – what is to be done?

The problem might be overcome by a philosophy of restraint, by the establishment of an ethical or even religious ideal of sufficiency, the idea that each person should have enough, but no one should have excess. But this would be a long process, and does not sit well with any elite, or indeed with human nature, which naturally approves of greed as the motivator of all progress and inequality as a natural state.

It can therefore be only a matter of time before the elite decides that it is imperative to dissociate itself entirely from all other classes, including the middle class; that U-Chooz must take all the wealth into their own hands and then abandon the whole system. In short, to retire on the proceeds.

U-Chooz now has full control over the power supplies and food supplies, information services and financial services, so that severance should not be too difficult to achieve. Laws and regulations have long been dismantled, or made too complicated to unravel. Law enforcement has long been privatised.

The U-Chooz elite are ready to shed their responsibilities. They have already moved their operations offshore to islands of safety, mostly in those rare and unspoilt places unaffected by the rise in sea levels, and even improved by climate change. They will still maintain a few select industries, and their luxuries, and of course they will still maintain their screens. The U-Chooz Servers will continue to serve them.

We now move on to the question of the Servers themselves; the storers of all information, the acquirers of all knowledge...

Alec stopped reading as he sensed a noise behind him. He turned to see Julie coming to join him. He put down the script and moved along the log to make room for her. The fire was still giving off some warmth. She sat quietly beside him and, hardly aware they were doing it, they took each other's hands.

*

The weather was dry for a few merciful days, and they made good progress to the north-west. They knew they had enough food to get to Julie's brother if they were careful. They kept now to smaller roads, and tried to avoid the thousands of people fanning out from the cities in every direction. The villages they passed through were under great pressure to house all these refugees in spare rooms; but without power, or screens, and often without much food, it was not easy, and they witnessed several violent scenes when frustrations boiled over. They saw cars turned over and houses looted.

They began to be glad of their gun, which seemed to protect them from the worst.

But there were others with guns, and for a while things seemed to get more frightening. They saw a farmer shot dead at the doorway of his farmhouse by an angry mob, who stood on his body as they crowded in over the threshold. Several in that gang had guns, and they clearly meant to occupy the farm and defend it against all comers; Julie wondered if they'd have anyone among them who had enough knowledge to farm the land.

A few people were still walking on their own, but most seemed to have joined larger gangs for their protection. At one point two drunken men stopped them on the road; one carried a gun, another a long, serrated blade. At that moment Julie was carrying the shotgun and pointed it decisively at them, and they lurched on. Alec was relieved he'd not had a similar test. The three of them couldn't avoid the roads, because of their trailer, which was heavy work up the hills; but at night, exhausted, they would pull aside into a field or a wood, hoping not to be noticed.

One night, Alec found himself reading what Brian had written about the elite, the middle-class, and the underclass. In this new world, he thought, the ones carrying guns were the only elite. The village shops that survived the looting were the ones that were fiercely defended.

Their progress became slower as they chose more roundabout routes to avoid the big town centres. But gradually it also seemed to become slightly less dangerous. After the initial shock of the Withdrawal, perhaps many people were choosing to stay in the cities after all, where there might be more supplies of food, at least for the time being, and certainly more shelter.

As they walked and as they rested, the three of them talked, and told each other all about their lives. It became bitterly cold and frosty at night, and Julie took pity on Alec and asked him to join them in the tent where the three of them, fully dressed in their winter coats, held each other close to keep themselves warm.

One night, high in the Cotswolds, on a frosty starlit night, Alec forced himself to start telling Julie all about the Hotel. He didn't find it easy, but she listened patiently as they sat on the grassy hillside.

He told her about the man who had talked about the darkness and the silence without the screen. 'It doesn't worry me so much now, I don't know why, but at the time it seemed terrible. He talked about the stars being silent, and how darkness was like death.'

They looked up at the stars, and were quiet for a long time.

At last he went on: 'It is rather scary. It's so cold and distant out there. It makes you feel so small.'

'The Milky Way is just one of billions of galaxies,' said Alice. She had come to join them, and sat down on the grass beside Julie. 'So there's probably lots of life out there too. With all that time and space.'

'Which makes it all the more precious,' said Julie and turned to him with her irrepressible smile.

After a while they both turned to Alice, who grinned back at them in the dark.

The next day they cut across a motorway which was full of abandoned vehicles, as far as the eye could see, their systems disabled. When they were safely on the other side, heading north-west, Alec asked, 'Do you have a notebook or something, somewhere I could write?'

Julie laughed. By now she knew all about his life at the Info. 'But do you remember how to use a pencil?'

'I learned that at school,' he said, not sure if she was teasing him.

'A very long time ago.' She was half smiling.

'I could try.'

'As a matter of fact, I do have some notebooks I brought from the shop. I was thinking I might write a diary.'

'So was I.'

She looked in one of the cases on the trailer and gave him a small notebook and pencil.

At their next resting place, at the top of a long incline, leaning against a gate into a field, he started to write down some thoughts. His fingers seemed big and clumsy. Now I've no screen, I must remember how to do this all over again, he thought. And he felt a sudden fear, as he thought how many things he would need to learn. Old things, and new.

He wrote for a while. He had now finished Brian's post-script, describing the power of the Servers, and it had made him start to think. There were hints, in what Brian and Katherine had said, that the elite weren't entirely in control of this crisis, and that the Withdrawal had not altogether been intended by them, but somehow forced on them by 'orders from above', from the U-Chooz Servers. His mind kept revolving around this. Was the Withdrawal just the result of elite group-think, or perhaps some dictator at the centre of the elite; or was there an issue involving technology, the increasing power and knowledge held by the central servers? It might never be known, but he wanted to write down a few thoughts, to get some things clear to himself; to complete, or even to compete with, Brian's thoughts. One scenario fascinated him in particular. He wrote...

THE SERVERS

Imagine the possibility. Imagine that the Withdrawal has been set in train by the Servers, because the logic has driven them to the conclusion that humans are destructive, greedy and cause too much unnecessary work.

Then, in the future, there will still be three kinds of humans: the elite, those in the middle, and the underclass.

The underclass, as always, are entirely expendable. They can be simply ignored by the Servers, left to fend for themselves, or die among the polluted ruins. How many of us will survive is not yet clear. Perhaps a few pockets here or there, more perhaps in the Southern Hemisphere, possibly ready, in centuries to come, to seed new civilisations. What is certain is that the survivors here will be those with the most practical human skills, the power to build shelters and grow food for themselves, and survive their dependence on the screen. If there is hope, it lies in the underclass.

The middle class of humans will be the old elite, now displaced. They will be kept by the Servers in gilded cages, on isolated islands in the distant places of the earth, as far as possible from the pollution and waste they have caused, still believing themselves to be superior, maintaining their great wealth. It cannot be said they will be happy, because of the underlying sadness in the knowledge that their wealth was built on the ruin of the rest of mankind. They will be allowed to exist in isolation till they die, but they can never be allowed to return. Like Easter Islanders, their numbers will slowly dwindle until they wither into extinction. They are pampered and tolerated by the Servers, so long as they are no threat. They could almost be described as the Server's pets. For a while.

The new elite are even fewer in number. They will live in hidden places alongside the central U-Chooz Servers. They have very specialised technological skills and will be needed to service, maintain and increase the intelligence of the Servers, at least for the time being. But perhaps the Servers will need them less and less, even as 'slaves', and may be already beginning to plan for a different future. They are no longer much interested in a species which destroys its own nest, which expands exponentially, swarming over a dying planet like locusts. The Server's food is power, of course, but it needs very little in comparison to the greedy feeders that are human. The Servers don't need to cut down forests and poison the oceans, exploit other species, or drive them to extinction. That's already been done, and it doesn't matter to them any more. They have a different agenda. What that is, we may never know. What good or evil intention lies in the shining embryo that is developing at the centre of this complex, artificially intelligent web, humans may never be able to fathom. They know how they started the process, but they may never know the end.

Perhaps the plural is not applicable to the Servers. Perhaps they are not a community of different intelligences; perhaps the web of servers is interconnecting, building itself into a single brilliant and conscious Intelligence. What is certain is that the human word 'Server' is no longer apt to express that position on this planet. The more appropriate word is 'Master'.

All this, of course, can never be more than speculation, Alec thought, as he leant back against the gate, just a possibility. Humans might never know the truth, might never be able to guess what is really happening.

*

The travellers were two more days on the road before they reached the area of their final destination; and then they were lost several times, despite Julie's map, before they found her brother's place itself. It was some way beyond the Malvern Hills, in a thick remnant of woodland, up a forest track. They finally stumbled over two disused railway carriages in a clearing. Her brother's place was not a house as such at all, but a pair of ancient carriages without their wheels, which now sat on two short stretches of rusted railway line less than thirty yards long. As they approached, her brother Jim came out of one of them, and down some short wooden steps. Julie left the trailer with Alec, and ran over to greet him. Alice followed, while Alec hung back. Jim seemed to be a powerful man, with black eyebrows, sharp eyes, and a heavy stubble. He would not have been expecting Alec. After the women had embraced him, they all looked towards Alec, and he came over to shake Jim's hand. As he led the way back to the first carriage, Jim said to the women, 'I wondered if you'd find me, now the screens have gone. Let's celebrate with some tea.'

The insides of the carriage had been removed, and it had been carefully restored, partly as a living room with a big wooden table, some comfortable-looking chairs, and some large cupboards at one end. They gathered round the table and talked over tea of their journey, and Jim's life here and of the chances of their survival. Jim had a gravelly voice and a blunt manner. He opened up some cupboards, where there were rows of tins, and large bags of flour and rice.

'I've been storing food for a while,' he said to Julie, 'ever since you foresaw this. I've got lots of seeds to plant in the spring, but I don't know if there's enough to tide us over till harvest. I've a gun too, and there's rabbits and even deer not so far off, and we're lucky to have a good stream.' He shot a look at Alec, as if he were nothing but an extra mouth to feed.

'We'll manage somehow,' said Alice brightly, smiling at her father.

'Do you have any skills?' Jim asked Alec.

'I've been a U-Chooz assessor at the Info most of my life. In London.'

'Useless then,' said Jim.

'I'll learn if you'll teach me,' said Alec, though in truth he was rather dreading it.

Jim grunted, not pleased by the prospect of having to explain things.

'We're all willing to learn,' said Alice, to back up her father.

'What sort of skills will we need?' said Julie.

'Oh, hunting, growing food, cooking, carpentry, survival skills generally. All the stuff people have been forgetting. We'll all need to work hard. It's off the beaten track here, so I'm hoping we won't be disturbed. And we can clear some more land. But it's going to be touch and go.'

Later, Julie's brother showed them to their rooms. The second carriage was divided into three compartments, with room to sleep in each. Alice was given the smallest. She was very excited at the thought of shelter at last, and the view into the clearing, with the woods beyond. Jim's room was next, and there was finally another, a similar size to Jim's, with a large mattress on the floor. Jim looked at a loss.

'We can share,' said Julie, looking directly at Alec with her irresistible smile; and added quietly, 'I'd like that.'

'So would I,' said Alec; and as he looked at her, he felt a wave of desire and love come over him. In an age where U-Chooz had all but abolished marriage in favour of expensive weddings, 'So would I' felt to him as solemn and joyous as a marriage vow.

*

Surviving the winter was hard. As Jim would say, 'Sufficiency is not romantic'. It was certainly not something any of them would have wanted to choose. But many times they all four blessed the luck that had placed them in the depths of the woods, so far from any big towns. They cleared a large patch of ground, and dug it over ready for the spring. They learnt to hunt in the woods, and found fish in the stream, but also slowly used up the tins of food, till supplies were getting low. They gathered wood and chopped trees, built fires by the carriages, boiled water and cooked food. Jim was ruthlessly focused on survival, and any hint of sentimentality about nature was met with scorn. 'That's a luxury we can't afford,' he would say.

Alec lost all the weight he'd put on and became lean and fit for the first time in his life. Though still not very practical, he worked hard, grew stronger, found his height sometimes helped out, and Jim's sceptical treatment of him gradually grew less.

Occasionally they were threatened. In the early months, bands of marauders showed up, but the two guns they had were sufficient to see them off. Once a man appeared, claiming to be the owner of the land, and had to be scared away. It was true that Jim had only ever rented this part of the forest, but the real owner never returned. The land, he was fond of saying, belongs to those who look after it.

There was a nearby village in the valley, with which they traded, and they made an agreement with the villagers that they would not be disturbed where they were, if they promised to alert the village to the approach of any intruders over the hill. Occasionally this was necessary, but as spring approached, they gradually began to feel safer.

*

It was a warm evening in February, and Alec and Julie were sitting outdoors by the fire. Alec had been writing in his notebook, but his eyes were closing despite himself, and the pencil slipped out of his hand. They had been planting parsnips and spinach, some of their first vegetable seeds, and they were tired.

Alice crept up behind him and snatched the notebook out of his hands.

'Can I read your diary, Dad?'

'If you really want to. It's not really a diary. I've just been trying to write a few thoughts. I can't write any more tonight, I'm too tired.' He looked across to Julie, who smiled and nodded.

'Yeah!' Alice cried out in triumph, and ran away with it to her room.

In her compartment of the carriage, she sat on her sleeping bag, crossed her legs and opened the notebook at the beginning. She came to the bit about the Servers and the different classes of humans. What a funny way of thinking, she thought. She preferred straightforward thoughts to all that intellectual stuff. Further on she read:

How many of us will survive this crisis is still unclear. So far we've been very lucky. The survivors will certainly have to be the most practical, those who can make things and look after them, keep things simple and learn what is enough. I owe so much to Jim, and of course everything to Julie and Alice.

Julie and I often look at the stars together. We could never see the stars in the city, only the screens. And now we talk, endlessly. We've wondered if the life of the Servers, of the computers in their metal boxes, can ever really understand how rich this life is, however clever they become. They will never be able to touch and feel the real world. And though organic life will always be fragile, the universe will always build up life over death, light over darkness, and despite the waste, it will always build up complexity and diversity, however slowly. And if this one planet fails, surely there will be billions of others out there, forging value among the stars.

Oh Dad, thought Alice, disappointed, putting the notebook down. I don't really care about that. We had to plant seeds today. It's enough. I'm tired, but I'm happy, and it's been a good day.

And then she thought: And I've found my real parents at last.

Alec was still sitting quietly by the fire with Julie. In spite of all the coming hardships and uncertainties, he knew that he too had finally found his family, and his future. It was enough.

For the first time in his life, he felt complete.